The Jungle Never Sleeps

J. R. Goodrich

Published by J. R. Goodrich, 2024.

This is a work of fiction. Similarities to real people, places, or events are entirely coincidental.

THE JUNGLE NEVER SLEEPS

First edition. October 7, 2024.

Copyright © 2024 J. R. Goodrich.

ISBN: 979-8227005342

Written by J. R. Goodrich.

To Cassidy, who first read my stories.

Chapter One

The day was new. Already, the jungle was a living, breathing thing. Three figures prowled the undergrowth, wolflike, lithe and silent but for the soft crunch of the forest floor beneath their boots. Leaves brushed against Jack's skin, cool and moist. A symphony of insects rang incessantly in his ears. Ahead of him, a Katydid fluttered through the gloom. It was dark. Though the sun above was bright, a thick canopy of leaves filtered out all but a few frail shafts of light from reaching the forest floor. Somewhere, a bird called, and another bird answered.

Jack could hardly see his own feet through the thick underbrush. There was a trail, yes; but not one that Jack thought he could pick out on his own, not even after a month of traversing these paths. He simply followed Kaskil. Close on his heels padded Flint. All three carried spears, their polished shafts slick with dew and the sweat of nerves stretched like guitar strings, their obsidian tips glinting even in the dim light.

Around Jack's neck, a pair of dog tags clinked softly. His brother's.

Kaskil held up his fist, and Jack came to a quiet halt. He turned his head; hissed:

"We're close. Not much further."

Jack gave a quick nod, then twitched as a bird rustled in the undergrowth beside him. Adrenaline spiked in his veins.

"Scared?" said Kaskil. He grinned his shark-toothed grin — each of his teeth was filed into a glistening point. Square-jawed and frighteningly blue-eyed, with a short, messy crop of sandy hair and a sturdy build, he wore a pink Hawaiian shirt with the sleeves torn off.

A deep scar ran across his face just beneath the eyes. It accounted for a sizable nick from the bridge of his nose.

Jack forced a smirk. "Just excited. I love this place."

"Hey," came a gruff voice from behind, and the prod of a spear tip. Jack turned, and saw Flint, his broad, hulking form hunched, his stony face hard-lined, his thick knuckles white around the shaft of his spear. On his right forearm, a wrist blade was fastened in its leather holster. Thin leashes led from the hilt to each of his fingers, to that the weapon was able to be unsheathed with a clench of the fist and held; when its grisly task was complete, the fingers could be straightened and the blade pushed back into its holster. A slouch hat was shoved down to his eyebrows. Palm fronds were lashed to his body here and there but did little to disguise his massive bulk. His eyes told everything; stormy, humorless, narrowed. "Enough of the chit-chat, or we'll have company."

Kaskil smiled, shook his head, and they set off again through the brush.

The time would come around eventually; each of them knew it, and that morning it had come. It was their turn to check the east trapline. The jungle was densest on the east side of the island, and worse, the bandits favored it for exactly that reason. Not only this, but their stronghold was situated on the east side of the island. Jack hated the place; dreaded even the mention of venturing into it. He hadn't once run into trouble since fate spat him out on the Island's shore, even whilst serving as a guardsman with Kaskil and Flint — but he'd heard stories. Of the bandits, in particular. They were vicious. Years of dispute over hunting grounds and border conflict had hardened general distrust into violent animosity. From there, the relationship between the two peoples of the island had spiraled into bloody chaos.

As a result, Jack had done his best to avoid being sent into the forest. Avoided it like the plague. Really, it *was* a plague, the way it crept into his consciousness, haunted him like a ghost. And enough ghosts haunted him to begin with.

But someone had to check the traps. Besides, he had Kaskil's bravado to buoy him.

They crept onwards for what felt like an eternity. Every tickle of a vine were the fingertips of a bandit, every nip of a mosquito: a poison dart. The insects' chatter was maddening. Unending. And it was hot; so, so hot. Every inch of his gray tank top was stained and plastered with sweat. His patched, ragged army pants were heavy with moisture. His jet-black hair, held up in a sloppy ponytail, felt like a wet rag glued to his scalp. Steam hung suspended in the air all around them as they stalked deeper and deeper into the jungle.

Jack could taste the humidity on his tongue. It filled his mouth, his nose, his ears. . . It was a solid, ever-present thing; suffocating; unceasingly damp.

Eventually Kaskil held up his fist, and the trio stopped. Jack felt a cool wave of relief wash over him. They'd reached the trapline at last; there, upon a vine-smothered tree trunk next to the trail was a carved symbol, half-draped in creepers: an 'X'.

"'X' marks the spot," Kaskil muttered, kneeling. He brushed aside the fronds of a voluminous fern, startling a stick insect from its hiding place. It flapped away into the gloom. Jack felt another surge of adrenaline, and told himself to relax.

Stay cool.

He leaned over Kaskil's shoulder as the blue-eyed man reached down and extricated an enormous rat from the trap. The creature was evidently well-fed, pot-bellied as a pig with a rich coat of brown fur. Kaskil, holding their prize in both hands, grinned. "Behold, the king of beasts. Radiation sure does wonders."

Jack smiled, if only a little. "Alright. Let's get to the next trap."

"Nerves gettin' to ya'?"

"Nah."

"Sure."

Jack stood and lent a hand to help him up. Kaskil ignored the gesture and turned to Flint, whose eyes never rested on a single spot of forest for more than a second. Kaskil pointed and asked the bigger man:

"The next trap's *that* way, ri–"

He never finished the sentence. A great crash erupted in the underbrush behind them and winged insects swarmed past in a desperate bid to escape. All three men spun, spears at the ready, as a man erupted from the wall of leaves, a knife glinting from one of his fists. He struck Kaskil like a wrecking ball and tackled him to the ground. Jack and Flint moved to help him, but two more interlopers lunged from behind, a crackle of branches giving their attacks away at the last minute. One of them lunged for Jack. He had no time to thrust with his spear before he was slammed to the ground and the man was on top of him, kneeling on his chest, his knife raised to strike. Jack lifted his hands to block it, but it was too late. He could only jerk his head to the side as the blade sliced down his cheek, drawing a line of fire and spilling sticky blood down his face and into his ear. His vision flashed red with pain, but, seeing the Bandit aiming to stab again, his hand flew up and latched into the man's wrist, blocking the attack. His other hand reached out to the side — grasped the head of his spear. He swung it sideways straight into the bandit's wrist. The man screamed and dropped the knife. Jack threw him off; tackled him, yet sloppily. The bandit's knee slammed upwards into his chest, knocking the air out of him and rendering him momentarily vulnerable. His attacker took the opportunity. He pinned Jack once again, and locked his fingers around his victim's throat. Jack punched and scrabbled furiously at the man's hands, but his grip was like iron. He reached out for his spear. Found nothing. Gone, too, was the knife. Panic gripped Jack's chest as it hitched emptily in an attempt to draw a breath. The bandit's eyes blazed — those of a madman — as Jack stared into his face. He could feel the man's hot breath. See his yellow teeth bared in a crooked grin. Jack's lungs burned. His windpipe ached as it was crushed like a soda can by fingers too strong to pry free. He kicked his legs wildly; his vision clouded; his lungs screamed for air —

Then his foot found purchase. The bandit's groin. He kicked with all his might. The man cried out and stumbled away backwards, his face screwed up at the sudden pain, doubled over at the waist. He looked at Jack, weaponless. There was fear in his eyes.

Finish him.

Jack leapt to his feet, spear in hand. He did not think. Only felt. His veins itched with molten blood; blood that surged through them like a fiery bore tide. There was only one thing left to do. He felt not an ion of hesitation.

He grunted and plunged the head of the weapon deep into the bandit's stomach. Twisted it. Stepped back. All at once, his enemy's face seemed to slacken as if the skin had come loose from its fastenings.

The bandit teetered back and forth, pawing uselessly at the wooden shaft emerging from his abdomen. Pink froth bubbled up between his lips. He looked at Jack; knew his fate was sealed, and there was a blank, sad kind of acceptance in his expression. The light drained from his eyes. The *fight* drained from his eyes.

Then, he fell.

Jack stared on for a moment at the corpse, breathing hard, then reached down and yanked the weapon free, feeling his stomach turn a bit at the sticky strings of gore fluttering like streamers from its obsidian tip. His chest still heaving, he turned to the others to assist them. But his aid was not needed. They, too, had dealt with their attackers accordingly. Flint's bandit sat crumpled against a tree, his shirtless torso streaming with shocking red. The big man was silent; stoic; grim. He wiped his wrist blade clean and pushed it back into its holster.

Kaskil behaved in the opposite manner.

"Stupid bastards," he sneered, grinning insanely. He drew a menacing bowie knife from his belt, crouched, and set about the process of beheading the dead body with the serrated side. Jack looked away. "Shoulda' known was what was comin' for 'em..."

"Kaskil!" Flint hissed. "Keep it the *fuck* down!"

Kaskil ignored him, sawing busily away at the neck of his attacker. He looked suddenly up at Jack, his irises flashing like shards of ice. His hands were shiny with the bandit's blood. It steamed as if so many rubies had been melted and spilled between his fingers. He grinned. Strings of spittle hung from his jagged teeth like cobwebs.

"First kill, huh?" he asked. His tone was shockingly jovial.

Jack hesitated a moment before responding. He felt giddy with adrenaline, yet somehow so fragile, as if, at any moment, he could be shattered into a million pieces. His head spun. Should he feel guilty? Proud? Should he feel anything at all? He just turned the corner of his mouth up a little (it was hard to do), and said, "Yeah, I guess so."

Looking down at his hands, he saw they were shaking.

"You ain't fresh meat any more, Jack!" Kaskil crowed, slapping him on the back. "You're one of us now. A *real* Guardsman." He turned to their sullen companion. "Right, Flint?"

Flint sighed and kicked the body of the man he had killed over into the grass. "Give 'im another week."

Jack looked down.

Kaskil gestured to Jack's cheek. "I see you've earned yourself a trophy."

Jack felt the side of his face, and his hand came away wet and red. Pain began to gnaw suddenly at the split flesh. His eyes teared up. Deep in his veins, the tide of adrenaline was receding; for a moment, he'd forgotten the wound. "Is it bad?" he winced.

"Terrible. Thank god you're not gonna' die without any scars."

This was little comfort to Jack.

Flint tore his spear out of his attacker's throat, and the man's body crumpled into ferns. He looked unamused as before. "Thanks a lot for all this, Kaskil."

"What?" Kaskil cried. "What'd I do? These—"

"You never shut the hell up. Always running your damn mouth." He shook his head. "You think I like this? They're bandits, yeah, but you think I like *killing*?"

Kaskil looked at him a moment, then stuck out his tongue. To Jack's surprise, he glimpsed the bare hint of a smile flicker across Flint's lips; there one moment, gone the next — his features were cold and hard once more.

"Well?" said Kaskil to Jack. "Go on, take his knife. It's yours now."

"Y-yeah." He reached down and retrieved the bandit's knife where it lay. Saw his own blood spattered on the blade. It was surreal. Unreal.

My blood.

"And his head," said Kaskil. "Take his head."

Jack shook his head weakly. "No, I can't."

"Suit yourself. Or you could strap a set on and do it."

Jack glared at him with an expression of disgust. "You're crazy. You're sick."

"*I* have a backbone."

"Yeah," Jack scoffed, looking away. "That's what this is all about."

"You two," Flint spoke up. He, too, carried the head of his opponent. "Enough of the chit-chat. Let's move out."

"What's with the hurry?"

Flint's jaw muscles clenched under his skin. "I won't dignify that question with an answer."

Kaskil grinned. "You'll lose your head in here sooner or later," he said, then laughed at his own joke. Flint did not. Neither did Jack.

They hefted their grisly prizes and headed off into the jungle towards home. Eli's dog tags jingled softly around Jack's neck as he walked. He wondered if his brother would be proud of him.

No.

First, Eli would have to forgive him.

Somewhere, a bird called, and another bird answered.

Chapter Two

The trio didn't walk long before they were met by another of their own. Dark-skinned and clad in old military fatigues, the leader of the guardsmen stepped into the path ahead of them and gave each a fresh burst of adrenaline.

"Jesus, Leto!" Kaskil shouted, his eyes wide, weapon poised. He chuckled and punched Leto in the shoulder. "Ya' wanna' get speared, or what?"

Leto smirked. "I'd like to see you try." He raised his eyebrows upon noticing what the three carried besides their spears. "Looks like you guys ran into some trouble."

"No no," Kasil chuckled, raising the head he held. "*They* ran into some trouble." The four of them, minus Jack, shared a laugh. Leto noticed the cut on Jack's cheek.

"Hey, Jack!"

"Sir?" Jack spoke up.

"For the last time, drop the 'sir.'" He pointed to his own cheek. "You've got a little somethin' there."

"It's just a scratch," Jack replied with a weak smile.

"Consider it a trophy. It suits you."

Jack smiled. "Thanks." He touched the wound gingerly. "Hurts like a bitch, though."

Kaskil grinned his bear trap grin. "Builds character."

"Did you kill?" Leto asked Jack, quite bluntly.

"Yes," said Jack in reply.

"Your first?"

Jack nodded.

"Good work."

Jack wasn't sure what to say. He didn't think he'd ever be congratulated on taking the life of another man. He just nodded again and looked down.

"You bothered much?" Leto asked him, crossing his arms. "I mean, you've only been here a few weeks."

Jack shrugged. It didn't matter if he felt guilty or not; it didn't matter if he felt anything — he'd made up his mind to appear as far from that as possible. "Not really," he said. "I mean, it was him or me."

Leto clapped him on the shoulder. "Tell yourself what you like. You're a cold-blooded killer now."

They laughed. Jack didn't.

Kaskil raised his free hand. "All right, all right, enough of the chit chat! I'd hate to have company."

"I'm sure you wouldn't," Flint muttered.

Kaskil elbowed him. "Oh, Flint, you never quit running your mouth."

With that, they set off. Leto accompanied them the rest of the way to the gate of the Fortress.

The Fortress was both a village and a redoubt. It was their home. The whole compound was surrounded by a high stockade of sharpened logs stuck vertically up and down into the soft soil of the jungle, and shaped like a hexagon if viewed from above. A rickety catwalk ran along its top. One side of the fort opened up to the beach; the other to the jungle — that was the side they approached from. As palm fronds parted and the gate loomed above them, topped by the propellers of long-doomed vessels, two sentries stepped forwards to greet them. Greetings were exchanged. The guards complimented them on their kills, then let the four men inside. Jack puffed a heavy sigh of relief as his boots met the hard-packed earth inside the stockade. Only when he was within those towering walls did he feel truly safe. He felt lighter, almost.

Kaskil scraped his shoulder on the frame of the gate as he tried to shove past Flint, and cursed. Jack turned to him, smiling.

"Builds character!" he said. Kaskil flipped him the double bird.

It was nearly midday, and all the villagers were up and about — all one hundred or so of them. People moved like a sea around their trio. The pleasant noise of human commotion, quite unlike the din of jungle insects, was music to his ears. It meant safety. Security. An anthill with none of the painful stings. The whole Fort was quite small, about two hundred paces in width, yet it was bustling with its inhabitants. Some prepared fish freshly hauled from the sea; others butchered deer and pigs; tended a small garden; hauled water; mended their clothing; still others washed it; spears were made; sharpened; patrols set out. Some went along the beach, and some ventured into the green hell Jack had only just escaped.

The villagers ranged in age from bumbling toddlers to old crones, but each was expected to pull their own oar in keeping the Fort alive. Most had come on the same old ex-troop transport on which Kaskil and Flint had arrived, the wreck of which now lay rusting and crumbling, pounded incessantly by breakers far out on the reef.

The Guardsmen, though, were the most revered of them all. There were thirty of them in total, operating in ten small units of three men. Jack, Kaskil, and Flint comprised one of these units.

Shelters were erected here and there to shade them all from the sun. And at the far end of the fortress's clearing stood a small hut fashioned from corrugated metal and crested by a crop of palm fronds. It was the finest structure in the place. This was the Captain's hut.

A small group of children scuttled past as they made their way to it, and Jack felt guilty that they had to see the wastes of conflict that Kaskil and Flint carried; however, the youngsters were enthralled. Jack felt a pang of sorrow for them. He'd grown up with comic books and television and baseball and apple pie. It didn't seem fair.

Flint ushered them on their way, scowling with annoyance.

As they crossed the clearing at the center of the fort, heads turned from every direction. Eyes of every sex, every age glued to them; stuck there. More and more villagers took notice of the victorious trio with each passing second. The chatter died down and was replaced by muttering. Thrilled muttering. Jack watched as people put down their occupations and looked up to see the gruesome parade.

He wasn't sure if he liked the attention — so many gazes were fixed on him. Too many. But he knew it was *good* attention. Even though his guts twisted anxiously with every step he took, he walked with his head held high. A smile teased the corners of his lips.

Leaving a wake of excited murmurs behind them, they reached the door of the Captain's hut and Kaskil rapped on the door. There came a muffled voice from within, then footsteps, and the door swung inwards.

The captain was a man of sixty or so years, with skin like oil smoke and hair the color of bleached whale bones. The scars of a few million smiles creased the edges of his eyes and around his mouth. He still wore his uniform and cap, albeit a bit ragged, and a pipe dangled from the corner of his mouth. He was never without it.

"Tell me, boys," he began in his thick Somali accent, "did the traps bring in a good haul?"

"Well," Kaskil replied, smirking. "We've got something else to show you."

The Captain squinted through his cataracts at what Kaskil held up for him to see. "*Mashalla!*" he exclaimed, grimacing. He did not look quite as pleased as Kaskil did. "Terrible, terrible. . . Alas, I can always count on you boys to keep us safe."

Kaskil beamed. "Thanks, brother. It's the least we can do."

"And not too badly hurt?"

"Jack got a bit roughed up."

The Captain grimaced. "Are you alright?"

Jack nodded. "Yes, sir."

THE JUNGLE NEVER SLEEPS

He received a warm smile. "I am glad you are finding your place among the Guardsmen. Proving yourself. Fitting in."

"I am, sir."

The Captain looked down at the head Jack held. "You are becoming a good fighter, too, I see."

Jack smiled and dipped his head politely. "Thank you, sir. I try my best."

"It is well enough."

Jack dipped his head again. He could never dip his head enough.

"Well, you three," the Captain continued, taking a puff from his pipe. "Take those... *things* from my sight. I must admit, I am saddened by the deaths of these young men, believe your victory is worthy of... a celebration, perhaps?"

Kaskil's face lit up. "Wow, sir! You really think so?"

"Of course. All three of you have shown great courage, and that should be rewarded. Made an example of. Besides, I am sure Flint is yearning for an excuse to share some of the fruits of his *distilling* labors."

Flint smiled. "Yes, sir. I'd be happy."

"I, of course, will not partake." He held up his hands and smiled.

Kaskil clapped him on the shoulder. "Always the virtuous one, aren't you, Cap?"

He chuckled. "Always." A rough semicircle of curious villagers had formed around the captain's hut, and he addressed them. "My people," he began in a louder, richer tone, "these three young guardsmen have done a great service to us all. A truly great service. They have risked their lives to protect us, our hunting grounds, and our sanctuary from the terrible men who threaten to destroy it. They have made fine examples out of themselves; fine examples." Jack felt color rush to his cheeks. "Therefore, I find it appropriate that tonight, we shall make merry for the sake of their victory!"

The crowd cheered. Even the most sullen of the villagers, those who Jack knew had seen their closest friends and loved ones taken by a world as uncaring as it was unforgiving, wore a glad expression. Jack felt all the happier for it. It was like cool aloe nectar spread on a sunburn. Yes, the nectar may soon dry up; the burn may have soon returned, but that was not what mattered at the moment.

Leto led he, Kaskil, and Flint out of the fortress, where they set the heads on long pikes and stuck them into the ground just outside the stockade like grisly totem poles. While Kaskil laughed as a honeysucker pecked at the oozing eyeball of one of the heads, Jack shuddered and turned away. He was glad to be rid of them.

A feeling of exhaustion soon gripped his body and mind. He didn't dare tell Kaskil or Flint, but he was thoroughly rattled. His temples throbbed. It was all too much. Hoping to avoid the bustle inside the fortress, he stole down the beach, slipped past the guards, and laid back in the sand at the base of a shallow bank where the beach met the jungle. An umbrella of palm fronds shielded him from the stinging sun. They swayed gently, like stage curtains. The shade was wonderfully cool. He took his hair out of its ponytail and kicked off his boots. There he basked, watching a heron pluck its way through the seaweed at the water's edge, the bandit's knife close at his side.

Out on the reef, breakers gnawed at the wreck of the *Luzon*.

Kaskil's words flashed in his mind — *You're one of us, now*. A real *Guardsman*. He ran them though again and again, savoring them, hanging on the end of each one. After all his training and hoping and suffering, the moment had finally come.

But it seemed only a split second later that Leto's words invaded his thoughts.

You're a cold-blooded killer.

Jack swallowed hard. Leto had been joking. But to Jack, that sentence rang all too true. He felt suddenly cold; colder than the shade could make him. A lump was growing in the pit of his stomach.

Kill or be killed. That was the old adage, wasn't it? It was him or the Bandit. And if earning the respect of the tribe meant taking another man's life, he reasoned, then so be it.

So be it.

A smile pranced upon his lips, but they suddenly twisted and tears came instead. They came hot and salty and fast into the dirty palms of his hands. He did nothing to stop them. He cried and cried until he had no more tears left to cry. For a few long minutes he simply sat, red-eyed and spent, staring out at the waves.

Jack knew it was all worth it. He'd always dreamed of being a part of something bigger. A part of something worthwhile. This was worthwhile, wasn't it? He couldn't name a single one of the villagers if he were asked, but he felt a magnetic sense of duty to protect them. He told himself that he couldn't explain this feeling; told himself it was nothing but the better angels of his nature, nothing but his conscience. Perhaps some inner sense of selflessness. But deep down, Jack knew this was a lie.

Wasn't he already a cold-blooded killer?

It hurt to admit, but what he felt was remorse. That was it. Pure and simple. Even as the thought crossed his mind, he could feel the cool steel of his brother's dog tags against his chest, a nagging reminder of what he had done, of his actions that stormy night that he would give anything to go back and undo.

There would be no undoing. That much was true. But if Jack knew anything, he knew that the future was malleable; his destiny was his own. Never again would he let the events of that fateful night be repeated. Never again would he let an innocent life slip through his fingertips like sand through a sieve. From the moment Jack joined Kaskil and Flint in the defense of their people, from the moment he hefted a spear and pledged his allegiance to their cause, he swore to be a protector; not a betrayer. A preserver, not a destroyer.

A guardsman.

It was only a matter of time before he felt his eyes closing, felt his muscles slackening. Sleep was not long in taking him in its icy claws.

Jack's eyes fluttered open, stinging in the sudden light. He licked his lips. They were salty.

All around, the sea murmured its greetings to the new day.

Wet sand had piled against his slumped body as if it assumed the worst and had taken it upon itself to bury him. Water swirled around his arms and legs with each incoming wave, jostling them about as if he were indeed a lifeless corpse.

He lifted his head. A battalion of palm trees greeted him from the crest of the beach, and beyond that, wrapped in the haze of late morning, a great peak rose from the jungle. He looked down the beach; saw figures — several. They stood in the surf, apparently searching for something. One picked up a life ring. Tossed it aside. Jack's blood ran cold as he remembered.

Remembered the roaring surf. The roll of thunder. The crash of splintering beams.

Suddenly one of the figures cried out:

"Look! That one's alive!"

The source of the voice, and several others, quit their occupations and splashed towards him through the waves. They held weapons.

Jack froze. He felt dizzy as they approached him. Should he run? Would they kill him? Who, even were they?

Eli was nowhere to be seen. Neither were their captain, their crew, their friends . . . all gone. He was alone.

Utterly alone.

As the men assembled before him, blurred and faceless, he felt his strength suddenly dissipate. The world swam. His blood turned to molasses, his neck to rubber, and as his face hit the wet sand, a curtain of darkness dropped down upon his stage.

His eyes snapped open to a bloodred sunset. A rill of cold sweat trickled down the back of his neck. As the memories came rushing back, he squeezed his eyes shut, feeling tears building up behind the floodgates.

My fault.

"Jack!"

He jumped and spun around, clutching his knife. Kaskil stood atop the bank behind him, smirking down, a bottle of Flint's moonshine in his right hand. "Jumpy as always." He tsk-d. "You're missing all the fun. I've been looking for you up and down the beach for *hours*."

Jack stood, smiling. "Hours, huh?"

"Hours."

"What was that about missing out on the fun?" Jack said, cupping his ear.

"Shut up," Kaskil hiccuped. "Let's get back to the fort, okay? God, you need a drink."

Jack composed himself, climbed the bank, and followed Kaskil into the night.

It didn't take long to find out that he wasn't missing much fun. On the other hand, Kaskil was having the time of his life, dancing close with their tribe's more promiscuous girls, the bottle never leaving his hand. He laughed — no, he *cackled* — unendingly. His teeth were red-hot nails glinting in the firelight. His eyes flashed, twin snowglobes of sparks. Flint stood at the far corner of the stockade, dispensing his questionably drinkable beverages to eager villagers, his stony features in shadow. Jack now held a bottle of it in his hand. It tasted like battery acid, and the bottle itself was encrusted with barnacles it had accumulated before washing up on the Island. He kept drinking anyway. It had been a long day.

A bonfire roared at the center of the Fort, and Leto sat before it on a barrel, guitar perched in his lap, his fingers flying over the neck, his voice soaring over the chatter of the crowd, all gravelly lows and teetering highs. Their fellow guardsmen gathered around him with drums. It was like a scene from a National Geographic magazine.

I wanna' be your lover, baby; I wanna' be your man —

It was pitch-dark but for the fire, and its eerie glow made the dancing villagers look like fiery wraiths, with Leto as their bellowing overlord. Their bodies were crimson flourishes of the Devil's paintbrush. They moved as one.

Tell me that you love me, baby; tell me you understand —

A pig, too, was roasting, but Jack had no appetite whatsoever. In fact, he wasn't sure *when* he would have an appetite again.

I wanna be your lover, baby; I wanna' be your man —

Eventually, Jack, Kaskil, and Flint were gathered up in the center of the Fort. Their names were chanted. Toasts were made. Backs were clapped. They were raised onto the shoulders of their fellow guardsmen and strutted about like parade floats.

Someone grabbed Jack's arm; raised it into the air, waved it around. He smiled and played along almost drunkenly as his name was shouted again and again like some pagan incantation. They grinned up at him and pumped their fists. Many of their names were still a mystery to Jack, but now they acted as if he was an old friend. It felt like a dream. Blurred. Unreal.

Jack should have felt happier. The others were happy. Happy for him. Happy that he had earned his place in the tribe, that he had helped to protect their home. That he had taken the life of another man.

And he *was* happy. Very happy. But the place was simply too much; it was loud; hot; *alien*. It was suffocating. At the first opportunity, Jack slipped away through the gate and out into the night silently as a cat.

Guards had been posted all around the stockade, but made no notice of Jack. They rotated in quick shifts to enjoy the celebration within, passing in and out of the gate with rapidity, clearly more focused on the commotion inside than on actually protecting the Fort. Jack stole silently past them and made his way down the beach to the water's edge. He stood there at the toe of the waves, letting his feet sink into the cool, wet sand. A gentle breeze ruffled his hair and clothing. It was quiet. Peaceful. Behind him, a glowing halo of orange rose above the palm trees, but the voices and the music and the laughter seemed far away. Jack turned his eyes out onto the horizon. A tiny sliver of red marked the sun's final resting place. He took a swig from the bottle and watched it fade slowly away into the inky blackness of night. A feeling of heaviness came over him all over again. He gave in to it, his rear plopping down in the sand as he allowed his eyelids slowly grow heavier and heavier. If nightmares wished to take him, so be it.

It was then that he noticed something.

A light.

A tiny pinpoint of white light, quite like a star, resting just level to where he figured the horizon ought to be. But it was not a star. Slowly, gently, it bobbed up and down as if carried by the swell. Jack felt the fog clearing from his mind as he realized that it *was* bobbing up and down with the swell. And it was growing brighter the longer he stared at it.

His anchor of drowsiness was quickly hoisted and he stood bolt upright, the bottle falling from his hands and landing softly in the sand at his feet. Up the beach he ran, squeezing past the guards and into the warmth and light and sound within. His eyes searched for Kaskil in the crowd. It was not a difficult task. He made his way through the crowd and pulled his friend away from the inebriated girl he was passionately kissing against the stockade.

"Kaskil!" Jack shouted over the din of the mob. "Come with me! I've got somethin' to show you!"

Kaskil scowled at him. "Can it wait, buddy? I'm in the middle of something here . . ."

"No!"

"Why don't you loosen up a little, co-"

"Listen to me, okay? You *need* to see this."

Kaskil's lips made a thin line. "Fine," he growled. "What is it?"

Jack stared at him. "Kaskil, it's a boat."

Chapter Three

Kaskil stumbled close at Jack's heels as they exited the Fortress. His prior ambitions were well forgotten. When the pair reached the water's edge, he splashed into the water and stood there knee-deep, staring out, as the light moved nearer and nearer, and faces, faint as mirages, began to appear in the recesses of its moonlike glow. The craft that carried them was now visible as well. It was small and frail with a tin shed erected in the center to shelter its occupants from the elements. A single pole stood in the center for a mast, upon which their light also hung. The light was electric, which Jack found odd, as electricity was a rare commodity.

"I can't believe it," Kaskil breathed. "Outsiders. Real outsiders."

"And a whole group," Jack added, incredulous.

"The last time . . ." Kaskil's voice trailed off, and he scoffed.

Swell after gently rolling swell drew the boat ever nearer until Jack could see the whites of the boat people's eyes, wide and fixed upon himself and Kaskil. Each of the outsiders was silent. Completely silent. They simply stared.

"Go!" Jack told Kaskil. "Run and get the Captain, and anyone else who's not too wasted to come down here!"

Kaskil bobbed his head, said "On it!" and vanished up the beach, leaving Jack alone as the Outsiders' vessel ground itself gently into the soft sand.

There were about twenty or so individuals in the boat. Their ages ranged dramatically, from toddlers clutching their mother's hands to old men stooped over like shepherd's canes. Some had skin like ivory, others black as the night itself. And still, not one of them spoke. They only stared.

Were they afraid? Was it fear in their eyes? Jack cocked his head. No; not fear. There was nothing. Their faces were strangely blank.

They must be in shock. Exhausted. Especially after such a long journey.

A too-long period of perfect silence elapsed before Jack raised his hand and beckoned them forth. "Come ashore!" he offered, unsure of what else to say. He did not expect the Captain to turn them away. "We ... We have food and water, if you need it!" Not one of them moved or spoke. He swallowed. "I won't hurt you! I promise." Nothing. "Don't be scared." Silence. His chest felt like a cave. "Please. Come ashore."

Just then, the sound of muffled, sandy footsteps approaching from up the beach could be heard, and Jack turned just in time to see the Captain, Kaskil, Flint, and Leto arrive. The Captain's eyes went wide as cannonballs as the boat people came within range of them, and his pipe nearly dropped from his lips.

"Outsiders!" he gasped. "I thought you were only playing a joke on me, Kaskil. But they really are Outsiders." He turned to them and lifted his hand in greeting. "Ahoy!"

They said nothing in reply.

"You must have journeyed far to reach us!" the Captain went on, unaffected. "If you are in need, we will make you feel right at home. We will do you no harm."

Finally, one of the Outsiders seemed to gather up enough courage to lift one leg and gingerly, ever-so-cautiously set it down in the swirling foam where the sea met the sand. The man, about thirty years or so of age, brought his other leg down alongside the first, and stepped forwards. He wore a checkered plaid shirt, well-patched jeans, and a short beard which was red as his hair. He was handsome. He spoke in a voice that was oddly melodic.

"Your hospitality would be greatly appreciated, my friend. We've come a long way, and have small children and old men and women with us. We have been in want of food and drink for many days."

The Captain smiled and bowed his head. "You and your people will be safe with us. Bring them ashore, and we will happily provide you all the food and water you may desire. I promise you this." He motioned up the beach. "We have a warm fire and hot food prepared as well, that I am sure will be found most agreeable by your friends."

The man smiled back and gave a dip of his chin. "I cannot thank you enough, sir. You are truly a godsend." He whispered something to a young woman still in the boat, and she in turn whispered to another man alongside herself. The three of them looked at one another, looked for another beat, then subtly nodded. One by one, helping their children and elderly down with gentle hands, the Outsiders exited their craft and assembled on the beach before Jack and his fellow tribesmen. They carried nothing with them but the clothes on their backs and their youngsters.

"May I ask your name?" the Captain asked the Strangers' presumed leader.

"Silas," he replied. The Captain offered his hand to shake and Silas complied, not before staring at the hand for a moment. Something told Jack it was a weak handshake, but he didn't blame the man; Silas must have been rattled from such a long time at sea.

Festivities wrapped up neatly as The Captain led his new charges up the beach and into the stockade. Eyes turned. Voices died. The music ground to a halt. For a moment, the drop of a pin could be heard. Then, as always with something new, there came the muttering.

Jack and his fellow guardsmen quickly put up a shelter for the outsiders along an empty section of the inner stockade, and they were thanked profusely, if a bit shyly. They huddled beneath their new shelter and eyed the bonfires with a funny sort of wariness. Many times they were offered spots around these fires, and each time they staunchly declined. Not even their children moved to soak up some of the fires' warmth.

Jack found them a bit odd, though pitied them more then he distrusted them.

But there was one thing about them that Jack found particularly bizarre. As he made his way to he and his units' hammocks near where the Outsiders were housed, he noticed the Captain offering them food and water. Silas, the man who appeared to be their leader, and had told the Captain that he and his people had been without sustenance for a long time, accepted it gladly. He took several deep gulps of water.

Then, as Jack watched from beneath a furrowed brow, he walked into the shadows at the back of the shelter and spat it all out. It gushed forth like a waterfall onto the flank of the stockade and pooled in the dirt below. The Captain took no notice. Silas looked quickly over his shoulder as soon as he was finished, as if he had meant to conceal the act, as if he had done something that was best not witnessed. Jack looked away quickly.

Maybe he wasn't thirsty.

But then, Jack's eyes grew curious and he looked back — looked back just in time to see one of the Outsider women, the fair-haired one whom Silas had spoken with at the shore, do the same, quietly regurgitating the water she had been given as soon as the Captain left and repeating the prudent over-the-shoulder glance.

Maybe she wasn't thirsty, either.

Jack dismissed the strange act, went to his hammock, and let the sound of chittering frogs lull him to sleep. He did not dream.

Chapter Four

Jack awoke early. Most of the other villagers had not yet stirred, and the night watch was just coming in through the gates to get a wink of sleep. The sky was a soft, dim blue, and in the air hung an early pall of wood smoke as Flint and Leto willed the previous night's fires back to life. In the distance sounded the faint roar of breakers.

Almost as soon as he opened his eyes, the memory of his fight with the Bandit gripped his guts and began twisting them into a tight knot. He tried to think about something else, but it was no use; every wall he put up against remembering the life drain from the bandit's eyes came crumbling down as if made of sand.

Staring but not seeing.

After wrestling with his thoughts for more than a few minutes, he accepted their presence and tapped out. He knew they'd fade as the day went on. There was no point in fighting them.

Yawning, he sat up in his hammock and stretched. He reached up and touched the cut on his cheek. It had scabbed over and didn't ooze anymore, but it was just another reminder of what he had done. It hurt less than the memories.

Kaskil's hammock hung alongside his, as did Flint's; units generally kept together and his was no exception. The fair-haired man was already awake and sitting cross-legged on the ground. On the back of his hand perched a positively gargantuan insect.

"What are you *doing?*" Jack hissed, wide-eyed. The thing was massive, larger than Kaskil's hand, with an orange-and-black segmented body and more long, spindly legs then Jack could count. Antennae the length of its body twitched from its head and from its rear. It held a cricket between its front pair of legs and was busily feasting away.

"Holding a centipede," Kaskil told him, matter-of-factly.

"Yeah, I know," Jack said. He racked his mind, trying to remember some thought tucked away far, far back in the dusty little storage units of his prewar mind. Then it came to him and he said, "Thereuopoda clunifera."

"Gesundheit."

Jack smiled. "Entomology major." He looked at the centipede. "Sadly, the world ended before I could get my degree."

"Entomology major — and bugs freak you out?"

Jack frowned. "No, but we studied that one and . . . I just don't like it. Too leggy. Too pinchy. Besides, those things are apex predators."

"Oh, yeah! I've watched them hunt before. Took a lot of inspiration."

Jack grimaced. "I think you're missing a few hundred pairs of legs."

"This one's extra big," Kaskil went on. "Must be the radiation, right?"

Jack scooted back in his hammock. "They only come out at night," he remembered, furrowing his brow. "This guy must like to stay up late."

He considered for a moment, then grinned. "I think I'll name him Larry." The centipede, as if had taken Jack's words as a reminder to get some shut-eye, hopped down onto the ground and skittered away at lightning speed. It squeezed into a gap in the stockade and vanished. Jack shivered.

"There's something wrong with you," he said to Kaskil.

"I know."

Jack fished a hair tie from his pocket and put his hair in a ponytail. He wondered if there were any more hair ties left in the world, as he'd inevitably lose this one. *I need a haircut,* he thought. "Sleep well?"

"Pretty well."

Jack paused, then leaned forward and said in low tone: "What do you think of them?"

"Of who?"

"Who do you think?"

"Oh, the Outsiders?"

"Yeah."

Kaskil scowled. "I don't like 'em. I don't really know why, cuz' they've got kids and old folks, but there's something... *off* about them." He shook his head. "It might just be my years in the jungle talking, but I don't trust 'em, man. I don't."

Jack shrugged. "Yeah. They're *weird*. But they seem pretty harmless to me."

Kaskil frowned. "I mean . . . you saw how they just *stared* at us from the boat. Didn't say anything. Just stood there, completely quiet — didn't make a sound. Gave me the chills."

"They were probably just scared. Or tired." He smiled. "We do live in pretty crazy times. Everyone's a little shaken up."

Kaskil tsk-d. "You're too trusting, Jack; I'm telling you. I've lived on this island a lot longer than you have, and I know better than to trust things I shouldn't. And I can tell when something's up."

"Come on, really?"

"I think so. I really do."

"What *do* you think?"

"I think . . . I think they're sick. They've got some kind of disease."

"Wouldn't they be, I don't know, coughing?"

"Maybe not. You don't always cough when you're sick."

Jack sighed. "I mean, I guess, well . . . I saw *something* last night that was pretty strange."

Kaskil leaned, elbows on knees. "Yeah?"

"Yeah." Jack proceeded to recount what he had seen the last night regarding Silas and the water. Kaskil shook his head upon hearing it, incredulous.

"You're joking."

"No."

"That's weird. Really weird. Weren't they thirsty?"

"They should have been, if they were without food and water for so long. And that's what Silas told us when they landed."

Kaskil's eyes lit up and he jabbed his finger in Jack's face. "See! I told you there was something going on. Maybe that virus of theirs makes their bodies think they don't need water. It dehydrates them without them even feeling thirsty. Makes them spit it out like it's . . . like it's battery acid."

Jack rolled his eyes.

"No, really! Whatever they've got makes them reject fluids. It dries them out; that's how it kills them. Like a mummy. Like a living mummy."

"Come on, Kaskil. How about this: maybe somebody gave them water beforehand and they didn't want to be rude when the Captain offered it to him."

Kaskil looked at him, smirking. "Sure."

"Well, I can't explain it any other way."

"I *can*. They're fucking weird, and they're *definitely* sick. So I'm just telling you, I don't trust them. And I sure as hell am not going anywhere near 'em."

Jack sighed. "Whatever, Kaskil." He paused. "Are they awake yet?"

"No," Kaskil replied. "But I've been watching them."

Jack turned to look in the direction of the Outsider's shelter. A funny idea struck him, so he gave in to it and counted the Outsiders. There were twenty. He knew they couldn't possibly be up to something nefarious, but it seemed a good idea to keep track of their number as he couldn't recognize them all by face or name.

Jack and Kaskil stared at the slumbering refugees a while longer. The group looked quite peaceful. A mat of palm fronds had been set out for them, and they slept close to one another like puppies gathered their mother. Then, as if stirred by some ethereal alarm clock heard only to them, each of the Outsiders opened their eyes and sat up at precisely the same time.

Jack looked at Kaskil, eyebrows drawn over widened eyes. "How . . . ?"

"Still don't believe me?" asked Kaskil, crossing his arms. "Explain that."

He received no answer. Jack could not find the words.

"Well, I don't want anything to do with 'em," mumbled Flint through a mouthful of venison. He, Leto, Jack, and Kaskil sat around one of the flickering campfires at the center of the Fort, turning their breakfast on sticks just above the flames like hot dogs. "I've never trusted Outsiders, and I'm not about to."

"That's what I've been tryin' to tell Jack, here," agreed Kaskil.

"I mean," Jack argued, "they're a bit weird, Flint, but do you really think we should have turned them away?"

Flint looked at him as if he'd asked the world's most pathetically stupid question. "*Yes.*"

"What have they done to you?" He frowned. "That's pretty heartless."

"I don't care."

"You know what I think, Flint?" said Kaskil. "I think they've got some kind of disease."

"Here we go again," Jack grumbled.

Kaskil repeated his dissertation on the Outsiders to Flint while Jack sat in scowling silence. He recounted Jack's story, their synchronous rousing, and his own theories on the matter, finally ending it with, "I'm not going within twenty feet of 'em."

"If I had my way," Flint said, "they'd be right the fuck back on that boat."

They looked to the fourth member of the group. Jack asked: "What about you, Leto? What do you think of our guests?"

Leto smirked. "I've got nothin' to say."

"Fine," Kaskil grumbled. Then, his eyes locked something behind Jack, and he prodded his friend. "Look. They're eating."

Jack swiveled his head and looked in the direction Kaskil pointed. The Outsiders still elected to avoid any open flame, and it appeared that their food had been cooked for them. Yet another puzzlement. Jack watched with a mixture of surprise and relief as Silas took a bite of the venison, chewed, and swallowed. Upon nodding to the others, they followed his example. Jack turned back to Flint.

"See?" he said, smirking. "They're eating just like we are. Nothing strange about it. Like I was telling Kaskil, somebody probably gave them water last night before the captain did. That's why they spit it out." He looked at Kaskil. "They do *not* have any kind of dis–"

"Look!" Kaskil hissed at him. repeatedly smacking his shoulder. "One of them's leaving."

Sure enough, one of the Outsiders — a girl about Jack's age, clad in white with blonde hair — got up and paced quietly to the fort's northerly gate, pushed it open, and slipped through. The guards, chatting as they changed shifts, made no move to stop her. She returned quickly and took her former spot around the fire. Jack and his fellow guardsmen watched, their meals forgotten, as another of the outsiders rose and repeated the act. He, too, returned promptly, and was copied by a third Outsider; then a fourth. The guards paid no attention to them whatsoever, and when they took their positions outside the gate, it seemed that each of the Outsiders was permitted passage.

Kaskil turned to Jack, smiling. "I bet I know *exactly* what they're doing."

Jack opened his mouth to speak, stopped, then said, "What?"

"Come on," Kaskil said, standing and walking away before Leto could protest. "Follow me."

Jack, equally curious, got up and followed Kaskil across the center of the Fort to the South gate, the entrance that faced the beach. Then, quietly and quickly, they snuck through as the guards changed shifts, and made their way around the stockade towards the north gate, hugging its outer wall as they did so. The two men stopped each time they reached a corner and peered around it. Finally, they came within sight of the sentries guarding the North gate. Along the trail heading into the jungle came one of the Outsiders, a boy of fifteen years or so, and the guards nodded to him as he returned. Then, as Jack and Kaskil watched, Silas emerged from the gate, and nodded to the guards.

"Careful out there," one of them could be heard to say. "You guys have the Runs, or what?"

Silas nodded solemnly. "It's terrible." Then, he vanished into the jungle.

Kaskil looked at Jack. "Sure he does," he said, smiling. They waited until Silas returned and passed back through the gate, then approached the guards. "Hey," Kaskil greeted them. "Gene. Tom."

"Mornin', Kaskil," Tom replied. He had short, brown hair, a pointed nose, and was built like a scarecrow.

"A lot of those new fellas' keep coming and going, don't they?"

Gene, a young and diminutive Korean, grimaced. "Yeah; apparently they've got a nasty case of the Runs."

"Well," said Kaskil. "Jack and I were just about to head out on patrol of the West side."

Gene raised an eyebrow. "It's your turn for that?"

"Yeah. Leto said so."

"Without spears?"

"We've got knives."

Gene shrugged. "Good luck, brother."

Kaskil saluted him. "Thanks." With a nod to Jack, he turned and jogged off down the trail. Jack followed close on his heels. He let himself glance up at the bandit's heads, still impaled on their poles, swarming with flies and sagging morbidly. He regretted it, still feeling more disgust than satisfaction at the act.

THE JUNGLE NEVER SLEEPS   31

Once they were out of sight of the guards and the jungle pressed in on every side of them, Kaskil slowed his pace to a walk, and began scanning the underbrush all around them. He stopped every now and then to run his fingers through the leaves. Jack followed him with his knife drawn, concerned less of the Outsiders' strange behavior and more of potential company.

Suddenly, Kaskil noticed something, and cried, "Ah-ha!"

Jack jumped. The jungle was getting to him, per usual. "*What? What is it?*"

"Look." Kaskil gestured off the side of the trail, where a clear path had been beaten through the ferns and bushes. He reached down and felt the stalk of a broken fern at the place where it had snapped. His fingertips came away wet, and not from dew but from pant secretion. "This is fresh. Really fresh. Come on." He beckoned to Jack and waded off through the brush, dew clinging to his clothes and hair. Jack took a deep breath and followed.

They didn't have to walk very far.

"Jesus Christ!" Jack uttered as he came to a halt alongside Kaskil, and a wave of pungent air hit him like a sledgehammer. He clamped a hand over his nose. Splattered across the undergrowth and tree trunks in front of them was a red-brown slurry of venison. Vomit. It was *everywhere*. Even the tree branches and vines ten feet above their heads dripped with it. Some it was barely chewed, as if the Outsiders had simply crammed it down their throats. Bucket's worth of the oozing substance were strung like spiderwebs everywhere Jack looked.

A long, quivering strand of the bile-soaked meat dripped down in front of Jack, missing his nose by a hair's width. "Ugh!" he cried, feeling his stomach perform a perfect somersault as he jumped away backwards.

Kaskil smirked and crossed his arms, shaking his head. "Thought so."

"God, this is disgusting!" Jack groaned. "They threw it all back up!"

"Just like the water."

"There's so much!" Jack exclaimed, feeling like vomiting himself.

"No kidding." Kaskil looked around, then grimaced. "God. Let's get outta' here. I don't want to run into one of those weird fuckers."

They crept quietly back to the fort, taking a brief detour so as to avoid the posted sentries, then slipped back into the South gate with a brief nod to the puzzled guards stationed there. Flint and Leto met them as soon as they stepped foot back inside the Fort, Leto looking less than pleased. He crossed his burly arms.

"Where the *hell* did you two go?" he said. "You just got up and left!"

Kaskil scoffed. "Come on, Leto. We can take care of ourselves. Now–"

"Let me remind you, Kaskil, *I'm* responsible for keeping track of my men. You follow *my* orders. I can't have any of you wandering off on me. What if we're attacked?" He jabbed his finger in Kaskil's face as he spoke, and Kaskil held up his hands.

"Listen, listen, okay?" Kaskil protested. "Me an' Jack followed their trail into the woods–"

"Unarmed, I assume?" grumbled Leto, pinching the bridge of his nose.

Kaskil ignored him. "Guess what we found?"

Leto let out a heavy sigh. "What?"

"One by one, they've been going back there into the trees and just *throwing up*. There's vomit everywhere."

"*Everywhere*," Jack attested, wrinkling his nose.

"Of course," Flint groused, his expression grim. "Maybe you're right, Kaskil. Maybe they are sick. All the more reason to get rid of them sooner rather than later."

"Well, one thing's for sure," Kaskil replied. "Silas told the guard that they all had the Runs, but they sure as *hell* don't have the Runs. From my experience, the Runs involve a lot more–"

Leto stopped him. "Yeah, yeah, we all know about . . . *that*. Listen, Kaskil. I'll make sure they're quarantined off from everyone until we can figure out what's wrong with 'em."

"I want them gone," Flint spat. "I–"

"Flint, I am not going to turn elderly women and small children into the jungle to die."

Flint opened his mouth, but Leto cut him off.

"That's the end of it."

He shut up.

"Now," Leto said to the three of them, "you've sat around enough this morning and done enough fucking off. It's your turn to hunt. Go get your bows and spears. Head down the beach to the west side where the river opens up, and sweep the marshes. Don't come back until you've got something big."

Jack nodded obediently, but Kaskil and Flint scowled at their superior. "Watch them, Leto," Kaskil growled. "Watch them closely."

"I will," was Leto's terse reply. "Now, get out of here before I have to go find the Captain. You've seen him when he's mad."

Reluctantly, they did as they were told.

Chapter Five

Rain fell, and fell hard. It plastered Jack's hair to his scalp; ran down the back of his neck and slipped into his shirt; somehow formed pools within his boots. The droplets grew larger and heavier by the minute, and their volume increased until the mountain at the center of the island faded into a pale haze; the line of trees at the edge of the marsh a mere smudge of green. The downpour slickened the branches of the snag they crouched within the weathered branches of. Jack looked down, wondering if the fall into the marsh below would hurt. It probably wouldn't. The reeds quivered as they were assaulted by the downpour.

"Go for it, Jack," said Kaskil, motioning to a deer grazing in the near distance. Though the branches that concealed the three hunters were stripped bare of their leaves, the deer made no notice of them, lazing chewing away at the green stalks all around it, totally impervious to the deluge from above. Once it looked up as a stork gilded softly past along the tops of the reeds, but soon resumed its meal.

Jack shook his head and looked down. "Ah, I dunno'. I always mess it up."

"Don't worry. Where's there one deer, there's gotta' be more nearby. Besides, you could use the practice."

Flint flared his nostrils. Rain dripped from the brim on his slouch hat. "Come on Kaskil, just take the damn thing. I'm sick of this rain."

"Oh, quit bitching. First it was the mosquitos, then a blister, then t–"

"I'm not bitching." He hunched his shoulders. "Fine, Jack. But you'd better not miss."

"No pressure," Kaskil snickered.

Jack hesitated. He sensed Eli's dog tags, cool and hard beneath his shirt, then sighed and said, "Okay. Give me the bow."

Kaskil handed the weapon to him. "Here."

"Wish it was a gun," Jack said, frowning.

Kaskil smiled and shook his head. "Nah. Guns lie to you. Bows tell you the truth."

"I guess," said Jack. "But I–"

Kaskil cut him off. "Just give it your best shot. If you can kill a man, you can kill a deer."

Jack smiled grimly. "You're on fire with the analogies."

"Get on with it," Flint grumbled, and Kaskil elbowed him.

"Bitching," said Kaskil. Flint seethed quietly.

Jack turned and began to climb down from the tree. The branches were like rocks coated in algae; slicker than ice. His knuckles went white around the dripping wood each time he stepped down to descend. He didn't look down. Just kept going; slowly but surely. He pictured himself slipping and tumbling through the branches, his body twisted and bent and battered like a ragdoll. He couldn't let a tree kill him.

Then, a branch broke. He yelped. Adrenaline surged in his veins, but fell only about a foot. He landed awkwardly in the mud with a splash. An embarrassed chuckle escaped his lips, and he sheepishly looked up to see Kaskil pointing in the direction of the deer. Flint glared down at him.

"*I see it*," Jack hissed.

"*What?*" Kaskil replied.

"*I said, I see it!*"

Kaskil cupped a hand to his ear. "*What?*"

Jack just gave him a thumbs-up and turned away. The reeds only came up to his chest, and his prey grazed a mere two hundred paces away, its tawny form obvious from where he stood. But now, the question was whether or not *Jack* would be obvious. Crouching low so that his eyes were only just concealed beneath the tips of the swaying stems, an arrow already nocked in his bow, he crept towards the deer. The reeds were soft as his footsteps. He made little sound as he approached it, though his boots sank to their ankles in muddy water with each step. The animal sensed nothing. Every few paces he stopped, muscles rigid, his breath halting, and began again. Still, the deer made no notice of him.

The rain began to abate. A gentle breeze picked up.

Jack came within fifty paces of the oblivious herbivore. He went down on one knee and raised his bow, squinting down the length of the arrow at his target's speckled flank.

And still, the deer did not move a muscle.

He pulled the string back. The bow bent. The obsidian arrowhead, sharped to a deadly point, yearned to fly. Eli's dog tags clinked softly together. Jack took aim.

Then the deer's head shot up. In an instant its legs became pogo sticks, and it darted away towards the safety of the trees. Jack's arm twitched, the arrow slipped, and it wobbled away into the reeds like a swallow with a broken wing. He cursed under his breath. Watched his quarry prance away.

Suddenly, the deer gave a strangled cry and fell. Jack stood up, bewildered; looked around. On the far side of the marsh rose the silhouettes of Kaskil and Flint. Kaskil waved to him — he still gripped his bow in the other hand. Jack sighed heavily and began trudging towards them. He wondered what Eli would have thought.

Next time.

When he reached the pair, Kaskil grinned his shark grin. "Alright, Jack. Tell me what you did wrong."

Jack slapped his arms to his sides limply. "What, Kaskil?"

"Temper, temper — come on, doncha' know?"

"I really don't."

Kaskil snapped off a reed and dropped it. It drifted with the breeze. "The wind."

"What about it?"

"It picked up as you were stalking the deer. And you came from upwind. Your scent was blown right into it."

Jack palmed his face. "Dammit. I did that *last* time."

"It's fine. The wind didn't start until it was too late."

"Well, good thing you guys went downwind and it got it for me."

"We expected something like that would happen," Flint grumbled.

Kaskil shrugged. "Yeah. You're still pretty new to this."

"It's fine," Jack conceded. "Bagged the thing one way or another."

They stared at the deer's carcass. Flint looked at Kaksil. "You gonna' carry it this time?"

Kaskil smiled, puffing out his chest. "You bet. Watch me." He hefted it onto one knee, struggled with it for a few moments, then slipped. It fell on top of him. "Get it off!" he wheezed. "God, it's heavy!"

Flint smirked smugly, reached down, and easily slung the animal across his broad shoulders as if it were a knapsack. "Quit bitching."

Kaskil got up, sopping wet, and glowered at Flint. "Yeah, screw you."

It was then that Jack's eyes caught a flash of movement in the distance, a blur of white against the treeline. A human. "*Get down!*" he hissed. "*Quick!*"

They did as he said and dropped to their haunches in the reeds, Flint still carrying their kill.

"What?" Kaskil asked in an agitated tone. "What is it?"

"It's a person!" replied Jack, pointing in the direction he'd seen the figure. "Look!"

They looked. Sure enough, a figure in a white blouse and skirt appeared to be running along the edge of the marsh. She stood out starkly against the dark green wall of trees behind her.

"It's a girl!" Kaskil muttered. "Wait, isn't–"

"One of the outsiders!" Jack exclaimed under his breath.

"What's she doing out here?" Flint said, flabbergasted.

Jack squinted into the distance. Something was strange about the girl. "Man, is she *moving*. I've never seen anyone run so fast."

Kaskil chuckled. "Wow, look at her go!"

The female outsider, the one who'd left the fortress first that morning, seemed to possess uncannily strong legs. They moved beneath her like a windmill in a hurricane. Her arms swung like those of a chimpanzee; her golden hair, though rain-soaked, still flowed behind her. It was almost a humorous sight. Jack could not tell exactly how fast she was going, but he was sure *he* couldn't keep up with her breakneck pace.

"What's she doing?" wondered Flint. "Running from something?"

Her head stayed almost perfectly still as he sped along through the reeds like a falcon on the hunt. She changed course slightly, angling towards a lone tree that stood apart from its brethren amongst the reeds. "No," said Jack. "She's *chasing* something."

"Huh?"

"Look."

Just as he said that, something leapt from the reeds just ahead of her towards the tree. It was a spotted wildcat — a Wildcat.

"A cat!" said Kaskil. "Why . . . ?"

"Shh. Just watch."

The creature leapt suddenly towards the tree, curled its forelegs around an overhanging branch, pulled itself up, and vanished into the leaves. But the girl wasn't about to give up her chase. She sprung into the air after it as if her legs doubled as jackhammers, launching her high into the air and she, too, vanished from their sight into the verdant folds of the tree.

"What the *hell*?" breathed Kaskil. "How'd she do that?"

Flint was speechless. Jack looked on in fascinated silence.

A struggle seemed to be ensuing within the tree. Branches and leaves twirled down into the swaying reeds below; boughs swayed; then, a piercing shriek rang out. The cry of an animal — it was not unlike that of the stricken deer.

"Don't tell me–" Kaskil began, but Jack held up his fist to quiet him.

The branches went still. No more leaves fell. Seconds ticked by.

Then, as if nothing at all had happened to it, the Wildcat crept out towards them on one of the tree's branches. It bore not a scratch — its mottled fur was not tainted by a single drop of blood. It tilted its head this way and that, leapt down into the reeds with its tail trailing behind, and was gone. The girl was nowhere to be seen.

The three men stayed down for a few beats longer, then Kaskil, grinning, stood. "Come on," he told the other two. "Let's go see what the crazy chick is up to."

"You kidding?" Flint scoffed. "I'm not goin' anywhere near a single one of those freaks. There's somethin' seriously messed up about them. I mean, she was chasing a damn Wildcat!"

"Exactly!" Kaskil proclaimed. "That's what's so *interesting*. You don't see that shit every day!"

"You said they were infected, didn't you?"

"I don't plan to get all handsy with her, Flint. We'll keep our distance."

Flint shook his head and sighed. "Whatever. But I'm leaving the deer here until we come back."

Jack stared at the tree for a moment. Tried to pierce the impenetrable shield of leaves blocking his view of what lay deeper inside. He bit his lip. Alas, curiosity was getting the better of him. Though his stomach felt a bit queasy, as if it could sense that something was afoot, as if it sensed something wasn't quite right, he couldn't help himself but indulge in his curiosities. Kaskil was right. This was far too odd an occurrence to walk away from. He had to look and see.

"I'll go," said Jack. "She could be hurt." Flint rolled his eyes.

"Sweet," said Kaskil. "Follow me; stay low."

They approached the tree in single file, keeping their eyes just over the tips of the reeds, bows in hand and nocked with fresh arrows. Not a single leaf moved on the tree as they neared it. The wind had died down as well. It was totally still. Like a small island amidst the mire of the wetlands, around the base of its trunk lay a ring of drier ground. They reached it with still no sign of movement from the tree. The three men circled its trunk, their weapons poised, and scanned the branches above. Little could be seen.

"Hey!" Kaskil called into the boughs. "You up there?"

"Are you okay?" Jack offered, feeling his stomach twinge. He raised the bow.

It's only a girl. She ran a little funny, but it's only a girl.

Flint gripped the trunk in his meaty hands and began shaking it. It barely quivered, but the motion was enough to dislodge a bird from its roost. It winged away with a squawk. "Hey!" he shouted, giving it another try. "Come down, ya' weird bitch!"

Kaskil reached up and shook a bough just over his head. "Yeah, come down! We won't hurt you!"

They called and called, flushed about every living creature in the tree, and saw nothing; heard nothing. The densely woven branches betrayed not a glint of golden hair, not a flash of bone-white fabric. The tree was empty. It became clear that if the girl *was* still in the tree, she was hell-bent on staying hidden.

Kaskil puffed out a breath and lowered his bow. "Well, looks like she's not coming down."

"Good," said Jack, backing away from the tree. "I dunno' why, but something about all this is giving me a bad feeling."

"I'm with Jack," Flint said, albeit a bit reluctantly. "Let's get out of here."

"Yeah," Kaskil agreed, still looking up into the tree. "I'll bet she turns up later."

"She'd better not." Jack noticed that Flint held his shoulders higher than usual; his neck stiffer. "Those people are trouble. I don't care how harmless they seem; you two saw the way she ran. It wasn't right."

"She ran like Bigfoot," Jack chuckled humorlessly.

"Exactly. I don't care what Leto thinks. I don't care if they've only been with us a single day. I've seen and heard enough already."

Kaskil rolled his eyes. "Oh, Flint. Always bitching."

They received a warm welcome back at the Fort. The villagers cheered the fruits of their expedition, and children swarmed them. Flint hoisted the carcass of the deer over his head for all to see as their fellow guardsmen moved in to congratulate them. Leto seemed more than happy to see them, a change of pace from earlier, and took the deer to be butchered. Jack still felt a bit dejected. Soon, though, he realized it was silly to feel sorry for himself any more. They would be eating well that night, and that was all that mattered.

Eventually the crowd dispersed and people went back to their occupations. Jack and his unit started to make their way back to their quarters when he remembered something. He stopped and found his eyes drawn to the Outsider's shelter. Sure enough, the fair-haired girl sat amongst them, casually weaving a basket from dried reeds.

"Hey!" said Jack to the others before they could walk away. They turned, and he jerked a thumb over his shoulder. "Look!"

Kaskil and Flint Looked. It was uncanny. The girl appeared completely unharmed. Her skin was clear; her hair untangled; her clothes intact. She turned her eyes up at them, and each looked quickly away.

"Well," said Kaskil. "I'll be damned."

Chapter Six

Jack awoke slowly. Something had stirred him from the depths of sleep; a tight discomfort in his lower abdomen was soon found to be the culprit. His bladder felt ready to burst. He knew he could wait until morning, could close his eyes once more and drift back into the cool, dark folds of sleep. He'd done it before. Besides, he hated venturing into the jungle at night. He hated the jungle, *period,* but night — that was the worst. It was thickest at night. Loudest. Darkest, obviously.

It felt the most alive.

Alas, his body begged him otherwise. Rubbing his eyes, which felt strangely dry, he sat up in his hammock and surveyed the interior of the Fort. Not a soul stirred. Everything was painted in the dreary silver light of midnight, or perhaps early morning. Very early morning. He stood and walked quietly to the gate. Night watches were posted there, so he spoke a few quick words with them and slipped outside.

The latrines were not far from the Fort. An orange plastic marker, colorless under the sepia wash of the moon, led him to a well-worn trail. He followed it. He walked quickly, hand on the hilt of his knife, eyes locked on the faint brown track of the path. His heart fluttered in his throat. He was reminded of visits to the basement as a child, particularly the dreaded return up the steps — a ghoul seemed to be always clawing at his heels.

A figure stepped out from the undergrowth. Jack gave a small yelp and drew his knife. Tom held up his hands; backed away.

"Whoah!" he gasped. "Jack, it's me!"

Jack exhaled and stowed his knife. "Jeez, Tom. Gave me a heart attack there."

Tom smiled and ran a hand through his hair. "Sorry," he chuckled.

"What are you doing out here?"

Tom looked around. "Oh . . . I lost somethin' earlier. A red bandanna. It was in my back pocket when I took a piss this morning, but now it's gone. I'm sure it's around here somewhere."

"Why don't you look for it tomorrow? When it's light out?"

"Leto already told me off earlier when I went to look for it. You know how he likes to keep track of us. I don't wanna' get on his bad side, see."

"I get it. I'm just out here to take a leak."

"Enjoy, I guess."

Jack chuckled. "Hope you find it."

"Thanks, man."

They went their separate ways. As Jack relieved himself into the latrine ditch, he could hear Tom wrestling with the ferns and taro plants alongside the trail, brushing them aside and pulling them free as he searched. Occasionally he cursed. Jack zipped up his fly and turned to walk back to the Fort.

As he did, there was a great crash amongst the undergrowth. Branches and stems and leaves were crumpled, crushed; torn apart. Tom gave what was perhaps a small cry, masked by the unending choir of frogs and insects that was like a blanket of sound draped over them. Jack felt ice water injected into his bloodstream. He drew his knife. It quivered in his hand as he advanced slowly towards the source of the sounds. There was a grunt from the bushes ahead. Jack froze for a moment, then moved forward. He brushed vegetation aside here and there, leading with his weapon, heart beating in his mouth. But after what felt like minutes, he found nothing. He was growing frustrated and afraid. He did not want to call for him.

But he did.

"Tom?" he hissed. The word barely carried through the cacophony of the night creatures. A bit louder: "Tom!"

There was no reply. Then, the undergrowth rustled again, this time much further away. Jack could make out a clear sound of footsteps tramping through the brush.

"Tom! You okay?" said Jack, properly shouting this time.

"Yeah!" was the reply. It sounded far away, but it was Tom, all right.

Jack smiled and shook his head, wiping the sweat from his brow. Nothing. It had been nothing. He was being silly; paranoid. The jungle was playing with his nerves. Tom probably tripped, perhaps skinned a knee, and got tangled up in some creepers. The foliage was like a snare sometimes. Jack continued on down the trail towards the Fort and reached it quickly.

The same two sentries stood by the gate. He approached them with a wave.

"Has Tom come through yet?" he asked the guardsmen.

The sentries exchanged a glance, then shook their heads. "No," said one. "He's still looking for the damned hanky, isn't he?"

Jack smiled and nodded. "Yeah. I'll bet it fell into the latrine."

The sentry gave a snort. "I don't doubt it. He ain't too good at keepin' track of things."

Jack bid them an uneventful night and they let him through. He padded silently across the fort to his hammock, careful not to disturb any of his fellow villagers. Somebody coughed. As he walked, and for no particular reason, his gaze drifted over to Tom's hammock. He stopped dead in his tracks. Tom was in it. Lying down, asleep.

He probably came through the South Gate.

Jack strode quickly across the clearing and knelt beside his hammock, feeling his heartbeat pick up again. He grabbed Tom's arm and shook it forcefully. Tom's eyes snapped open and he glared indignantly at Jack.

"Wha-what?" he mumbled.

"How'd you sneak past the guards?" Jack asked him, incredulous. Tom looked puzzled. "What do you mean?"

"Well, did you find it?"

Now, he looked even more confused. "Find what?"

"Your handkerchief," Jack spoke, his expression now matchin Tom's. "The red one."

"I don't know what you're talkin' about." He flared his nostrils. "Lemme' sleep, will ya'? I was having a good dream." He crossed his arms and rolled over.

What?

For a moment Jack stayed put, his mind a hornet's nest of questions, mouth-half open as if preparing to speak. But he didn't. There was nothing to say. Instead he swallowed, stood, and went straight back to his own hammock. He lay down and tried to put it all out of his mind, to stop thinking and get some rest, because none of it made sense in such a bizarre and unsettling way he couldn't quite put his finger on. But rest would not come easy for Jack. There was that usual uneasy feeling in his gut, and it stayed with him until sleep finally came.

Chapter Seven

The next day dawned, and Jack awoke to a rockslide of memories. He thought about the strange Outsider girl. About Tom. About killing the bandit.

His brother's face, contorted in fear, as the sea took him.

Jack stopped thinking. He sat up; rubbed sleep from the corner of his eye. He felt the cut on his cheek, and was relieved that the scab was undamaged. The last thing he needed was an infected wound. Kaskil was awake first, as usual, staring in fascination at his centipede as the creature devoured a grasshopper. He turned his eyes up to the Outsiders from time to time. Jack said nothing, simply met his gaze and nodded, then turned in the direction of their slumbering guests.

"Eighteen," Jack uttered.

Kaskil released his insect and moved to sit beside Jack. "Two down from yesterday."

"You counted them, too?"

"Of course. I'm surprised *you* did."

They watched the strangers rise in perfect synchronicity, just the same as the previous morning. Kaskil shook his head when Jack looked at him. His lips were a tight line.

And just as the day before, they exited the gate one after the other to empty the contents of their stomach after eating. They'd done it at dinner the prior night as well, according to Gene. Silas had told him nothing of any missing members of his clan.

Though the Outsiders appeared to have neither kept down a single morsel nor swallowed a drop of water, their strength and spirit remained impressive, not only evidenced by the Wildcat-pursuing girl.

They felled trees with ease, and carried them as if they were hay bales. They hauled water like the buckets were empty. Even the children kept themselves busier than those native to the Fort. As a whole, they were incredibly industrious, helpful yet almost entirely silent. Only Silas spoke, though sparingly.

Leto had done nothing to quarantine them.

"I've had enough," Flint proclaimed as they finished breakfast. They'd told him of the Outsiders' change in numbers. Jack had said nothing regarding Tom's forgetfulness. "I've talked to the other guards, and they're all suspicious. There's something wrong with them. Besides, they're wasting food." He cast the deer bone he was gnawing on into the fire. "We're going to Cap and reporting all of this. That's the end of it."

Jack shrugged. "They've barely been with us for two days, Flint. They haven't done us any harm. Besides, they're a big help. I say we wait."

"Jack," protested Kaskil. "You've said it before; it's better to be safe than sorry."

Flint nodded. "I'm not waiting for *our* people to start vanishing, too."

Jack stood. "Listen. I'll ask Silas if any one of 'em's missing. If he lies, then you're right — they're up to no good, and we can tell Cap."

"Do it. Either way, we're going to him as soon as you come back."

"Fine."

Jack turned and made his way across the Fort. He drew a deep breath as he walked, steeling himself for the encounter. He was more scared than he wished to be. His fellow guardsmen roamed the Fort all around him, but that fact didn't stop a chill crawling up his spine as he approached the Outsiders, who sat cross-legged in a circle under their shelter. They sat with their backs perfectly straight and muttered amongst themselves. Upon noticing Jack, their eyes swiveled in their sockets and locked onto him.

Jack, with a maelstrom of butterflies in his stomach, made his way over to Silas and knelt beside the man.

"'Scuse me, sir," he said after clearing his throat, trying to keep a waver from his voice. The Outsiders were still staring.

Silas turned his head, and smiled warmly. He somehow didn't smell like vomit. "Yes? You're Jack, aren't you?"

How does he know that?

"Um . . . yes, that's my name."

"Is something the matter?"

Jack felt his palms sweating, and not from the rising heat of morning. "I just . . . well, you should know that I care a lot about you and your people. I feel bad for you all. Really. You've been through a lot, and I don't want anything bad to happen to you."

"That's very kind to say."

Jack forced a smile. "Thank you. But, as I was saying . . . I've been pretty worried about one of you guys getting lost. Especially your little kids. So . . . well, I counted you all. And I counted twenty yesterday." He paused. "Today, there's only eighteen of you."

Silas stared at him for a moment, then rose. Jack stood alongside him. "Well," Silas replied. "I guess I'd better count them myself."

He took a moment to do so. The others seemed not to notice their conversation; just stared ahead unblinking into the gray matter behind Jack's eyeballs.

Staring but not seeing.

Silas finished and turned to Jack. "Eighteen; as usual. And I don't seem to see anyone missing." He looked back to his clan and cleared his throat. "Folks, would you mind looking around and seeing if we've lost one of our number?"

They did so, breaking their trance — to Jack's relief — and muttering to one another. Mothers counted their children. Friends whispered in one another's' ears. A verdict was soon reached.

"We're all here," said one of them, the girl in white.

"Nobody's missing."

"Nobody."

Silas turned to Jack and grinned. "Look at that! A false alarm." He put his hand on Jack's shoulder. His grip was quite firm, but Jack didn't flinch. "I want to thank you for being so considerate, Jack. This is a strange new place for all of us. Your kindness is *more* than appreciated by myself and my people. In fact, your entire tribe has shown us remarkable hospitality in only two days. I cannot thank you enough. I mean it."

Jack smiled back. This time, it felt more genuine. "Thank you, sir. It means a lot to hear that."

"Of course."

"And," Jack added, "I hope you all get over your food poisoning sometime soon. I've had the runs before. Terrible."

Silas grimaced. "Terrible is not a strong enough word, my friend. But, thank you."

Jack grinned and nodded. "Any time, sir. Get well soon."

"Many thanks."

He turned and walked away, feeling a little twinge in his chest. Was it guilt? Maybe. Although he had willed himself not to let them, Silas's words warmed something inside of him. The look in his eyes was almost fatherly.

But Silas had lied.

For some reason that was beyond him, the Outsiders had lost two of their group and somehow did not recognize the fact, or chose to ignore it. But why? Jack was certain he had counted twenty before. He'd counted more than once.

He returned to the fire and stood before Kaskil and Flint with his arms crossed and a pensive frown tugging at the corners of his mouth. He kicked a twig with the toe of his boot. "Silas lied," he said. "I mean, they *all* lied. Said not *one* of them was missing." He puffed a breath out. "You were right."

"Of course," Kaskil replied, nonplussed. "What did you expect? If one of us was missing, we'd report it to Cap, or Leto. They must be hiding something."

"But *what?*" Flint wondered. "What the *hell* could they possibly be doing that for? A blood feud? You think they killed one of their own, or something?"

"I don't know," said Kaskil. "But *I* counted twenty." He looked at Jack. "And *you* counted twenty." He shrugged. "I know what I saw."

Jack nodded slowly and looked at the ground. "And now . . . eighteen."

Flint stood. "Come on, we're telling Cap about all of this."

"Yeah," agreed Kaskil, who got to his feet also.

Jack moved his jaw back and forth in thought. There wasn't much of an option after all he'd seen. "You're right. We have to."

Flint grinned. "Glad we finally talked some sense into you. Let's go."

They crossed the center of the Fort headed for the Captain's hut, taking care to avoid Leto on the way, knowing their friend and commander would send them off on a mission before they could get within a hundred feet of the Captain. He didn't notice them passing by.

The trio reached their Chieftain's door and Flint rapped at the hardwood, which was still emblazoned with the title '*S.S. Luzon*' in faded letters. Footsteps resonated from within. The doorknob twisted with a sound akin to an angry parrot, and it swung open. Out stepped the Captain, grinning broadly as usual, and he looked the three men before him up and down.

He was without his cap.

"Good morning, boys."

Jack felt his breath hitch in his throat at the sound of his leader's voice. Something about it was wrong. Very wrong. "Uh . . . Sir?"

"Yes, Jack?"

His brow furrowed and he opened his mouth to speak, but Kaskil cut him off.

"Your accent, Cap!" Kaskil laughed, a tinge of discomfort in his voice. "It's gone!"

The Captain arched an eyebrow. "What do you mean?" he replied.

Jack furrowed his brow. The Captain's accent was back. It was the same old choppy Somalian inflection, like a sprinkle of some exotic spice over every word. And yet, for a handful of words it had been gone, and he had spoken in perfect english.

"Oh," muttered Jack, perplexed. "Nevermind, Sir."

Kaskil looked at Jack, then back at the Captain. His eyes glinted with curiosity. "Cap, your accent was gone. Just for a moment."

"Yeah," Flint chimed in. "Your English sounded incredible!"

"I've . . . never heard you talk like that before."

The Captain made a confused expression. "Boys, you must be playing tricks on me. You know my English is not so good. I do not know what you speak of."

"But . . ." Kaskil protested. "You . . ."

"Really, I do not know what you mean."

Jack gave a short, uncomfortable chuckle, at a loss for anything else to say. There was a long period of silence filled only by the chatter of the Fort as it slowly came to life.

The Captain cocked his head. "Is there something you have come to tell me, boys?"

Kaskil spoke up. "Well, we've just been paying attention to the newcomers, and–"

"Aren't they nice?" interrupted the Captain, smiling. "We truly have done them a great service."

"About that," Flint began, his features grim. "That may not have been such a good decision."

The Captain's smile vanished in an instant. It was as if his cheeks had been suspended with magicians' strings, and those strings had been cut clean through. "What seems to be the problem?" he asked. "Are they bothering you in any way?"

"No," Jack said quickly. "Not at all, sir. We've just seen some things that are . . . *odd*."

"Please, explain yourself."

"Well," Jack began, feeling the blood pool in his feet. "They throw up anything we feed them. Water, too."

The Captain frowned. "What they do after eating in their own private business."

"Isn't it strange, though?"

"Not in the slightest."

Kaskil scoffed. "Cap, they do it after *every meal*. They haven't kept down a single morsel of food while they've been with us."

"It's a waste," added Flint.

The Captain set his arms akimbo. He regarded them coolly. "Boys, it is not for you to decide whether or not these people should want sustenance. Perhaps they simply do not feel the urge to eat or drink." He paused, then added. "Perhaps they are tougher than the three of you."

Kaskil looked legitimately offended. "Cap, that's absurd! In this heat? They'd all be dead by now without water, and pretty weak without any food. But even their children are strong enough to do the Lion's share of work around here. I don't get it."

"Exactly," the Captain snapped. "They are more of a help to our tribe than any of you are. So why do you question their ways? We helped them in their time of need, and now they are returning the favor. I see no problem with that."

"But–" Jack began, and was promptly cut off.

"That is enough," the Captain replied sharply. "You will not speak of these people any more in such a manner!"

"We weren't–"

"That means *you*, Jack." Jack felt his stomach sink at being reprimanded. "This is unacceptable. Our guests are harmless and generous. I am disappointed that you would even think to come to me, and complain about them." He sighed and looked down. Not one of them spoke. "Leave my sight."

Kaskil frowned at his leader's words. "Cap–"

"You will address me as 'sir' from now on, Kaskil. Now *go*."

With their tails between their legs, they slunk off.

"What was *that*?" Kaskil said, incredulous. "He's never talked to us like that before! He *likes* when I call him 'Cap'!"

"And his accent," Jack agreed.

Flint looked concerned. "He wasn't himself."

"Hey, you three!" Leto called. They stopped and turned to see him hurriedly making his way toward them, shimmying through racks of drying meat and shouldering past villagers. He reached them, smiling, and opened his mouth to speak, but Kaskil growled:

"Not now, Leto."

He and Flint stormed off. Jack stayed. He looked at Leto, and Leto looked at him.

"What's up with them?" Leto chuckled humorlessly, his brow knit. "Did I do something?"

"No," Jack reassured him. "Don't worry. It's just . . . it's the Captain."

"What about him?"

"He was acting strange."

Leto arched an eyebrow. "How so?"

Jack told him all that had transpired. Leto crossed his arms. "Huh," was all he said. "As much as I'm annoyed that you three went to the Captain, I gotta' admit, that doesn't sound like him."

"I know. It's weird. Not just the Captain, but *all* of it." He looked at the Outsiders, who were milling about near their shelter. "Didn't you say you'd quarantine them? In case they were sick?"

Leto scoffed. "Oh, I just told Kaskil that to make him shut up — like giving a baby a pacifier. But now . . ." He scuffed the dirt with the heel of his boot. "Now, I think I will. As much as I hate to admit it, Kaskil was probably right. They've *got* to be sick. I mean, what else explains it . . . *any* of it?"

"They should be dead," said Jack.

"Listen," Leto told him. "I'll make sure they're kept away from the others, and I'll try to get them to drink something. That's the least I can do."

Jack thanked him. "Talk to the Captain too, will you?"

"I can't promise you that."

Jack grinned. "Later," he said with an awkward half-wave-half-salute, and jogged away.

"Wait!" Leto shouted. "Your orders . . . !"

But Jack was already gone amongst the villagers. Leto cursed under his breath and set off in search of Flint and Kaskil.

Chapter Eight

When Leto rounded the three of them up and gave them their orders, Jack was able to hazard a guess as to where they would be sent.

Back to the jungle.

It was always the jungle. Jack wondered if he, Kaskil, and Flint were being punished as they trudged along a narrow, muddy path that wound its way towards the West side of the Island. That morning it was just as dark, damp, and swelteringly hot as it always was. Steam rose from the broad leaves of palms and ferns all around them like dry ice in a cheap horror movie. Sunlight filtered through the thick canopy above in golden shafts. It was nearly midday, and already Jack's tank top was soaked through with sweat. He took a swig from his canteen as he walked, his trusty spear held in the other hand, the bandit's knife tucked into his belt. Eli's dog tags were like metallic wind chimes as they dangled from his neck.

The west side of the island was less dangerous than the east. But it wasn't safe by any means.

Jack led the patrol. He bore not only the unsavory responsibility of clearing cobwebs — and taking the occasional Orb Weaver to the face — but of scanning the trail ahead and remaining constantly watchful. It was difficult to see more than twenty feet or so through the thicket. His days of staring at the back of Kaskil's loud, pink-flowered shirt and praying for the best were over. It was the first time he'd acted as their unit's spearhead. He felt equal parts proud and uneasy. He wished he felt braver. Even though he had a weapon and knew how to fight, none of those things provided him comfort. He wondered if Kaskil was just as scared as he was. Wondered if he was just acting.

"You guys ready to kick some ass and take some names?" Kaskil chuckled from behind. Flint smacked his shoulder and shushed him. Jack said nothing.

They had been trekking for at least two hours — soon it would be time to turn back and make their second sweep on the way home. Jack was finding it difficult to stay alert for so long. In the oppressive, wet heat and suffocating greenery it was easy to succumb to tunnel vision.

Then he saw something. Something out of place.

He held up his fist, signaling the others behind him to halt.

"Watch my twelve," he spoke softly to Kaskil. He knelt before a fern alongside the trail and grasped one of its broad, serrated leaves. Squinted. Tiny drops of red were sprinkled across the leaf. They were stark as the first stars in a twilight sky. "Blood. It's blood."

"Fresh?" asked Flint quietly.

"Yeah." Jack rose, gave the signal to move, and the trio proceeded along the trail at a more cautious pace. Jack's eyes scanned the undergrowth all around him as he walked, searching for signs of a struggle.

He found those signs almost immediately.

A low-hanging branch: snapped in half and hanging like a broken limb; a taro plant beside the trail: crushed flat; another fern spattered with blood — this time, there was much more blood. But it was not only on the fern, for, as he walked, it seemed each step revealed more of the crimson fluid marking the vegetation all around him, spattered through the foliage like the brush strokes of some avant-garde artist. He could smell it. And now he could see footprints. Whoever had left the blood behind had been running — no, not just running, but *scrambling*. Fingerprints dug into the mud here and there. One handprint was filled with a pool of red.

He swallowed a lump in his throat. Something was wrong. Very wrong. He could hear Flint and Kaskil's breathing grow more and more tense by the second. But couldn't bring himself to stop, couldn't bring himself to turn back. He *had* to keep going.

Here was another puddle of blood.

And another.

And another.

Here was a boot. He didn't check to see if there was a foot still inside, but the boot was splattered in blood. He grit his teeth and kept walking.

Another puddle of blood. This blood was thicker; darker.

It's everywhere.

Another boot.

A leg.

A—

Kaskil's hand clamped over his shoulder. "*Jack!*" he hissed.

Jack's head snapped up. A gasp escaped his throat and he stumbled backwards, nearly knocking Kaskil to the ground. There in the middle of the trail lay a bandit.

At least, it had been a bandit. The only word Jack could think of to describe him was *mangled*.

His clothes were shredded. His arms and legs were twisted at grotesque angles, and one was completely severed. His attached hand still gripped a broken spear. Across his stomach and chest ran long, jagged gashes; gashes like those made by the claws of a bear.

"*My god,*" Kaskil breathed behind him.

Jack couldn't bring himself to speak. Though he willed them not to with every atom of his being, his eyes drifted down to the yellow-and-red slurry of the bandit's pulverized organs splattered all around his body like a hellish pinata. Nothing was recognizable. He felt vomit rise in his throat. Skin was peeled back everywhere on the man's limbs, exposing shockingly red muscle. His face was soaked in blood from a window into his brain. Mouth, cheeks, and brow were limp; slack; rather, it was his eyes that screamed a thousand screams. They bulged from their sockets, twitching. It was clear that he was beyond the realm of pain. His mouth opened a fraction. He struggled to speak; let out a few pathetic croaks.

Then, finally, a single word came out.

"Run."

And just like that, Kaskil's spear was protruding from his eye socket. Vitreous fluid ran down his face like snot. His broken body convulsed, then went still.

"What'd you do that for?" Jack uttered through clenched teeth. His stomach did a barrel roll as he spoke, and he fought down a tidal wave of bile.

Kaskil looked at him, his features hard-lined. "Put 'im out of his misery."

"The only good bandit," Flint recited from behind, "is a dead bandit."

"Who the hell did this?" said Kaskil, sounding both disgusted and impressed.

"Not a man," replied Flint. "It couldn't have been. See the claw marks?"

"Oh . . . those aren't *claw* marks."

Jack felt his breath catch in his chest. The shadows of something that might have been fear lingered in the irises of Kaskil's icy eyes.

"We shouldn't be here," Jack managed to say, his voice wavering. "We need to leave."

Kaskil smirked. "C'mon, Jack. It was probably just one of our guys." He looked at Flint. "I'm thinkin' it was Gene." He laughed at his own quip, but Flint did not. "That little Chinaman has a mean streak like nobody."

Jack started backing away. He looked between Kaskil and Flint, searching their faces. "Didn't you two hear him?"

Kaskil stared at him blankly and cocked his head. "Hear who?"

"The Bandit. Before you killed him, he . . . he was trying to say something. To us."

"Yeah?"

Jack cast a cursory glance over his shoulder. "*Run.* He told us to run."

There was a moment's silence. Tension hung in the air like electricity. Jack felt his heartbeat picking up.

Kaskil gave another chuckle, though this one sounded less sure of itself. He tapped the head of his spear against the ground. "Uh . . . Flint?" he said.

"Huh?" replied Flint quietly, staring at the corpse, sounding as if he hadn't heard.

Kaskil furrowed his brow, opened his mouth, closed it, then said, "Did Leto send anyone out here before us?"

Flint looked at Kaskil, his eyes dark and troubled. He slowly shook his head.

A beat passed.

"Those claw marks," said Jack, feeling twitchy. "Do you think that a wildcat . . . ?"

Kaskil shook his head. "Come on. Cats aren't that big." Flint shot him a hesitant look, and he smiled uneasily. "Right?"

"Don't be so sure of yourself," Flint told him. "I've seen mutants out here. Big ones." He paused. "And I mean, *big.*"

"Oh," Kaskil said.

A pause.

Kaskil raised his eyebrows, clapped his hands together and looked between his comrades, backing away from the dead bandit. "Um . . . well, we should be leaving."

"Now," Jack concurred.

"Quickly," Flint said, following suit in his friends' retreat. "Very quickly."

But just as they turned to quit the scene, something caught Jack's eye; something that shouldn't have been there. His heart was thundering in his chest, but he had to check it out.

"No, wait!" Jack insisted, stopping them. They looked at him quizzically as he knelt before the Bandit's corpse, every nerve in his body begging him to run, but his mind holding him fast. Trying to avert his eyes from the gore oozing from the man's shredded abdomen, he pried the spear from the man's fingers; held it forth for them to see. "Look."

"Great," Kaskil said, and gave a small shrug. "Now, let's get out of here."

Jack held up his hand. "No, Kaskil! Wait. Look at the head." It was slathered in blood, but Jack willed himself to touch it in order to pull free something wrapped around the point. He held up a small piece of torn fabric for them to see. It was half-soaked in blood, but the other half was unmistakable. The sight of it disturbed Jack even more than the sight of the Bandit's still-twitching brains. "It's *plaid*."

"So . . .?" replied Flint. Kaskil looked unimpressed as he looked agitated.

Jack shot them a frustrated glare. "Really? Come on, think. Who do we know that wears a plaid shirt?"

A beat passed before the realization hit them like a diesel train. Jack could see it in their eyes; it was a widening not unlike the bandit's in his final moments.

"We need to get back to the Fort," Kaskil spoke. "Fast."

Chapter Nine

Jack ran like he had never run before. His feet pounded the earth like a steady drumbeat, his breath ragged, Kaskil and Flint close on his heels. His veins pumped battery acid. Leaves and twigs tore at his skin and clothing, but he barely felt them. He only ran.

Eli's dog tags bounced against his chest.

Too late. We're too late.

Suddenly the North Gate loomed through the greenery and Jack picked up the pace, his muscles screaming, his lungs burning. The gate was unguarded. His guts twisted.

They crashed through the gate and into the Fort, foaming at the mouth, spears poised to attack—

Then, nothing. There were no screams. No cries for help. Blood did not stain the hard-packed earth. Villagers stopped what they were doing and met them with confused stares. A brief silence descended over the entire Fort. The new sentries eyed them questioningly as they changed shifts and passed through the still-shuddering gates. Then, in no time, the usual sounds of the Fort at midday resumed and their grand entrance was forgotten.

The adrenaline subsided from Jack's veins and he lowered his spear. Kaskil and Flint did the same. A cool tidal wave of relief crashed over Jack. He closed his eyes and let out a heavy puff of air, wiping sweat from his brow with one hand.

Thank God.

Gene approached them with a wave of his arm. "Hey, you three! You won't believe what just happened."

Kaskil grinned wearily and ran his fingers through his spiky hair. "We probably will."

"It's Silas," Gene told them, his boyish features poised in excitement. "He came through the gates only a little while before you three got here. Bleeding and everything. Says he killed a bandit that attacked him!"

It was insufferably hot, but Jack felt a cold chill slither down his spine. His fears were confirmed. He swallowed. "He did?" Jack managed in a small voice. "Was he ... wounded?"

"Oh yeah. He took a spear through the arm, but he's alright. Tough bastard."

Jack looked at Kaskil; looked at Flint. Flint clenched his jaw.

"He's right over there," Gene continued, pointing. Sure enough, Silas sat slumped against the stockade, one of the guardsmen and the Captain's doctor tending to his wounded arm. His plaid shirt was torn and bloodied. Flecks of brown were scattered across his face like freckles. Nearby, the Outsiders were gathered in full force around their leader. Jack quickly counted them; including Silas, there were only seventeen. He swallowed. "Everyone swarmed him right off the bat," Gene went on, "but Leto broke up the crowd. You missed the rush." He chuckled. "People love blood. Really."

Kaskil's blue eyes were dark; a stormy sea. "Where's Leto?"

"Oh ... over by the Captain's hut, probably."

"Thanks, Gene." Kaskil clapped him on the shoulder and took off in a hurry across the fort, pushing villagers aside and upsetting a barrel of water along the way. Jack and Flint followed close on his heels. Sure enough, they found Leto near where he was said to be, conversing with another of the guardsmen. Kaskil quickly dismissed the boy he was talking to with a shove about the shoulders.

Leto spun his head towards them, his golden eyes burning. "What was that for?" he snapped. "You can't just—"

"Leto," Kaskil said in a measured tone, looking him dead in the eye. "We found something. Something . . . *crazy*. Just listen, alright?"

Leto crossed his arms. "Fine. Make it fast."

"You know what Silas did, right? How he killed that bandit?"

"That was brave of him," praised Leto with a nod. "He's one of us, now."

Kaskil hesitated. "Well . . . *we* found the body. And it was . . ."

"Dead, I assume?"

Flint chuckled darkly. "Oh, it was *very* dead."

"Good. Just as Silas said. I'm sure he'll be glad to know his kill was confirmed."

"No," Jack interjected. "He wasn't just dead. He was . . . *shredded*."

"What's the problem with that?"

Jack grimaced. "Leto, it was barbaric." He searched for the right word, but something else was bothering him. There was something strange about Leto. "Inhuman," he said at last.

"Perfect." Leto turned his chin up. "It's what the bandits deserve."

"He was chased down like an animal, Leto," Flint said, stony-faced. "This wasn't in self-defense. You know our orders are only to act if we are attacked first. But, Silas . . . well, I've never seen or done anything like that before, and I've killed scores of the bastards. Do you really see *Silas* doing that?"

"He told us that he was attacked."

"That's not what it looked like."

Leto crossed his arms. "Accusing a man of defending himself, huh? That's real noble. If I'm not correct, the three of you took down your own number in bandits only a few days ago. You got a party. Did *I* reprimand you? Did I?"

"This . . ." Kaskil chuckled, shaking his head. "This is not what you think."

"Since when has it been wrong to kill a bandit?"

Flint scoffed. "That's not what we're trying to tell you. It was–"

"What *are* you trying to tell me, Flint?"

"He . . . he had *claw* marks on him. All over him. His skin was just torn apart like paper!"

"Claw marks," Jack emphasized, looking Leto dead in the eye. "Like an animal leaves. Not a human."

"That sound like self-defense?" Kaskil scoffed. "For God's sake, he was missing an arm!"

Leto raised his chin. "Just shows what a fighter he is."

"Leto!" Kaskil snapped. "Listen, you nimrod. I've never seen those kinds of wounds before from a human. His guts were like *jam*." His eyes bore into Leto's. "We're telling you, Leto, something's going on. Something we've never seen before."

"Nothing's 'going on,'" Leto sneered. "I can't believe you three. Silas fought well and took down one of our enemies. His victory should be celebrated–" He looked accusingly at Jack. "–just like *yours* was."

"A human didn't do this!" Jack argued.

"Then *what* did? Huh? *What* did?"

Jack was at a loss for words. "I don't know."

Leto sighed and pinched the bridge of his nose. "How do you know this was Silas's kill, then? Could've been an animal."

"Jack found a piece of his shirt on the end of the bandit's spear," Kaskil told him. "It was him. I don't know how, but it was him."

"So, you're saying it *wasn't* a human, but it *was* Silas?" He laughed, making Jack's skin itch. "You three need to drink some water. The heat must be getting to you."

Kaskil stepped closer to Leto and crossed his arms. "We're not fucking with you, Leto. This is serious."

Leto narrowed his eyes at Kaskil. "There is nothing 'serious' about an honorable kill in the defense of our people. I'm sick of you three going after our guests like dogs. All you do is accuse them of this; of that."

"Oh, please. We've already gotten this lecture."

"They've done nothing wrong. They're helpful. They're strong. You three'd better back off, or there's gonna' be trouble."

Jack furrowed his brow. Confusion roiled in his chest. "That's not what you said this morning."

"Oh yeah?" He cocked his head. "What'd I say, Jack?"

Jack swallowed. He'd never spoken to Leto like this. "You said that you agreed with us. That they were dangerous."

Leto looked genuinely shocked. "I *never* said that. Enough of this nonsense."

"You don't sound like yourself, Leto," Kaskil interjected. "You–"

"I sound exactly like myself, and I never spoke against our guests!"

"Really, Leto? You told me *this morning* that you were worried. That you'd keep an eye on them. That they were dangerous."

"I told you, I never said *anything* like that," Leto snarled at him. "*Nothing*. That's my final word on it." He leaned closer, jaw tightened. "You'd better watch how you speak to me. Just cuz' you've killed one Bandit doesn't mean that you're not still an Outsider to some of us. Now I'm not gonna' tell you again: I *never* told you that."

Jack felt a fire ignite within him — injustice, confusion. He couldn't stop the flames. Wouldn't. "That's a lie."

Leto raised his eyebrows. "Is it, now?" he scoffed. "A lie?"

"Why, Leto? Why are you lying to me? What did I–"

"If you accuse your superior one more time–"

"Liar!" Jack gritted out between his teeth, his fists balled. "You're a liar! You're putting us all in danger! You–"

"One more time, Jack! On–"

"You're a fucking liar!"

Leto's fist met the side of his face like a sledgehammer. Sparks flew across his vision, and his head snapped to the side as his commander's knuckles sent shockwaves running down his neck and spine. The pain was incredible. He slumped to the ground, groaning and clutching his face as blood trickled down from both nostrils and his ears rang.

Fury burned in his chest — an inferno. It was hot. So hot. He could kill Leto. Could strangle him to death. He watched through blurred vision as Kaskil stepped forward and sent his fist flying into Leto's gut. Leto fought back hard, Flint attacked him, and soon it took four of their fellow guardsmen to pull the three apart. Jack tried to get up, to help, but dizziness overcame him. He watched the world around him begin to swim.

Then he fainted.

Chapter Ten

Jack woke up to a throbbing headache. His left eye was nearly swollen shut, and he could taste dried blood when he licked his lips. He was lying in his hammock. Flint and Kaskil's hard-lined faces hovered just above his, and their features lit up when he came to. They sported bruises as well.

"Look who's awake," Kaskil said, grinning. "You were out cold for hours. We thought we lost you for a sec."

Jack forced a smile and sat up, a wave of pain bubbling up inside his skull as if it were a witch's cauldron. He drew a deep breath and clutched the side of his face. "Ah–"

Flint clapped him on the back. "You'll pull through."

"What–" Jack began. "What happened?"

"Leto happened."

Jack massaged the side of his face and flared his nostrils. "I remember now." He looked at them, feeling the ghosts of his rage momentarily swirl around his head before fading away. "What was wrong with him?"

"Leto?" Kaskil licked his lips. "I don't know. He wasn't himself."

"Yeah," Jack winced, looking up at them. "This morning he told me he agreed with us. About the Outsiders." He shook his head and closed his eyes. "It's like he was different. A different person. He even spoke differently."

"Like the captain," Kaskil said.

"Like the captain," Flint echoed.

Jack turned his gaze towards the Outsiders, who had retreated to their enclosure with Silas to pretend to eat dinner. It was evening. "There's seventeen."

"Three missing," Kaskil muttered.

They sat in silence for a moment.

"It's like they've got the Captain and Leto under some sort of spell," Flint sighed.

"God," groaned Kaskil, massaging his own bruised cheek. "Don't make me think about it any more." He looked at Jack. "We brought you something to eat."

He handed Jack a brick of venison wrapped in a palm frond. Jack smiled, and said, "Thanks."

"No problem."

He ate, and they watched the Outsiders.

Night fell quickly. The sky turned purple, the air cooled, and frogs began to chirp. A Flying Fox wheeled above the campfires' glow. Jack's head still pulsed with pain. He was exhausted. The memories of the bandit's mangled corpse should have haunted him, but sleep came almost as soon as he closed his eyes.

It was night.

The deck of the Luzon pitched and heaved violently like the tail of an angry serpent beneath Jack's feet. He secured the loose hawser and began fighting his way back to the cabin. Its portholes glowed through the lashing rain like eyes. The deck shuddered and rolled, and Jack was thrown to the spray-slick planks. A cascade of water poured down onto him as a wave crested over the vessel. He rolled in its current like a cord of driftwood. He could feel the uneven planks of the deck skipping along beneath his fingers; there was nothing to grab ahold of; nothing to stop the inevitable.

Then, a sharp tug at the nape of his jacket, and he jerked to a halt. The water receded all around him as if parted by Moses. He gasped for breath; looked up at Eli's face. It was stark with worry.

"Come on, Jack!" he shouted over the screech of the wind. He helped Jack to his feet, slung an arm over his shoulder, and the two stumbled their way to the cabin door. Eli twisted the handle and they lurched inside.

It was dim and yellow and stale within the cabin. A single yellow light swung like a pendulum from the ceiling, counting out time like a crazy metronome as the Luzon tipped onto its beam ends and forced every occupant of the cabin to brace themselves against its cramped walls.

The captain stood to the front of the cabin, his grizzled face pressed to the porthole, his jaw set. The wheel was lashed in place by several belts, but he held it in place nevertheless. His knuckles were white.

Six others occupied the cabin. Two were shadowy-browed men who spoke little and observed everything. There was a mother, a father, and their child. And there was an old man who was quick with words.

Eli looked at Jack. He had a sharp jaw and a crooked nose, broken by the butt of a Soviet rifle. "You okay?" he asked breathlessly.

Jack wiped the water from his eyelashes. "Fine. Thanks, Eli."

"Just don't go out there again, okay?" Eli chuckled.

Jack smiled. "Someone had to secure the rope."

"I could've done it." He put a hand on Jack's shoulder, his other hand against the wall. "Don't leave the cabin again, okay?"

Jack looked at him. "Okay."

A split second later, the sound of twisted, tearing steel thrust itself against the eardrums of every occupant of the cabin. They were thrown violently against the wall.

There were screams. The light shattered. Darkness enveloped the cabin.

Then there came water, cold and dark; water rushing in from every direction; water–

Jack awoke with a strangled gasp, sitting bolt upright in his hammock. His shirt was soaked with sweat. It was pitch dark.

A cold pang of grief struck him in the gut. It nearly doubled him over. He held his face in his hands, readying himself for tears, but none came. He sighed shakily.

"Bad dream, huh?"

Jack jumped; turned to the sound of the voice. His eyes struggled to adjust in the midnight gloom, but eventually they revealed Flint's hulking form perched at the edge of his hammock, forearms resting on his thighs.

"Oh," Jack chuckled softly, then chided himself for his edginess. "Flint. You're up late."

Flint raised his eyebrows and smiled. "I don't sleep."

"Nightmares, too?"

"You get the idea." He paused, shifted his jaw back and forth. Kaskil snored loudly alongside them. "I was in the war, you know."

Almost subconsciously, Jack reached into his shirt and grasped his brother's dog tags as if they had somehow sprouted legs and wandered off. They had not. He ran his fingers over the tiny embellishments in the cool steel like a blind man reading braille. "So was my brother," he said, nodding.

"I take it you weren't."

Jack shook his head. He felt a bit guilty in the presence of a veteran who wasn't family, and wondered if he should apologize. All he said was, "No."

"You're one of the lucky ones." He stared off into the murk behind Jack for a long beat before finally continuing. "It was... well, it was hell. I bet you've heard that cliche a lot, huh? 'War is hell.'" He scoffed. "It's a cliche for a reason."

"I believe you," Jack replied simply.

Flint paused, then said, "I bet you expected something different. I don't blame you. I did, too. We all grew up with war movies, didn't we?" He chuckled. "Oh, those Hollywood actors sure were heroes. Their adventures were every boy's dream. They were my dream. I'll bet they were your dream." Jack smiled a bit and nodded. "But . . . it's not like that. It just isn't." He licked his lips. "There was no *honor*. No morals. No heroes. Nothing. Just a contest to see who could end the world fastest, like some sick game of tug-o-war."

Jack was silent.

"I've killed more men than I can even remember. Past a certain point, it's all a blur of blood and bodies and bullets. But some things stick out." He looked down at his hands. "It was, uh, '61, '62 — hell, I don't remember. We were in the Cascades. It was midwinter. Freezing." He took a deep breath. "We came up to this Red camp. But we didn't have to do much to take it, 'cuz they were dead. All dead. Frozen. Except for one.

"I remember him crawling towards me through the snow. He pressed his forehead against the toe of my boot. He was begging; pleading. I couldn't understand a word of it. Then he looked up. I saw his face. So young. I–I'll never forget it. Couldn't have been more than seventeen." Jack could hear him grind his teeth and saw him ball his fists. "My Lieutenant made me shoot him." He gesticulated with a finger. "Right. Between. The eyes."

Jack was silent. Flint was silent. The frogs and insects chirped on and on apathetically. A bird called into the darkness, high-pitched and grating. Jack wished they would all just shut up. Shut up for just one damn moment.

"I'm sorry," Jack eventually brought himself to say.

"It's alright," Flint told him, smiling. "I lived through it, and that's what matters."

"I guess so."

"It's been a few years. I've forgotten the feel of a gun. The smell of the metal. The smell of the smoke. But the sound . . . the sound it makes when it takes a man's life? That sticks with you, Jack. It does."

Jack said nothing. He'd never shot a gun in his life.

"Nothing fazes me now," Flint carried on in a solemn tone. "Nothing — well, 'cept for the jungle." He smiled. "But I paid the price. My brain, it's like... it's like my own personal torture device. The nights are the worst. I can't escape it."

Jack scoffed and shook his head. "I thought *I* was messed up."

"Oh, we're *all* messed up, Jack," Flint chuckled humorlessly. "All of us. Our whole generation. Hell, maybe the *last* generation. *Ruined*." Jack stared at him through the darkness. He sighed, ran a hand down his face. "Can't do nothin' about it."

There was a pause. Then, Flint cleared his throat and said, "I've, uh, never told anyone about that winter before. I guess *I'm* sorry if it put you off."

Jack shook his head. "Don't worry. I'm glad you told me."

Flint smiled. "Sorry if I'm a dick sometimes."

"I get it," said Jack with a shrug. "I'm still new to the Island. Still–"

"No. Don't say that. Never say that." Flint put his hand on Jack's shoulder. "You're not an Outsider, Jack. Leto's not in his right mind. You're one of us."

Jack smiled. "Thanks, Flint."

There was a pause, then Flint asked him, "What's your story?"

Jack felt his stomach sink.

Tell him.

"My story?"

"Yeah. I told you mine. Now tell me yours."

Jack looked away.

"I mean, we found you washed up on the beach, so you gotta' have some kind of story."

Jack licked his lips. "I– I don't have a story. Really." He found it difficult to meet Flint' shadowed eyes. "There's nothing worth talking about, anyway."

Flint shrugged. "Fine. Keep your secrets."

"I mean it."

Flint just smirked and laid back on his hammock. Jack sighed, closed his eyes, and did the same.

They didn't speak any more after that; just swayed back and forth in their hammocks and stared at the stars, so far away, so alien yet somehow so familiar, like a million tiny eyes frozen in time.

Sparkling with tears.

Chapter Eleven

The next morning was long, hot, and slow. It hadn't rained for days and thick motes of dust hung in the air inside the Fort. Buckets of water, carried mostly by the Outsiders, were clustered in the center of the Fort. They were emptied again and again.

Jack and his unit had been put about the invigorating task — punishment — of fashioning spears, arrows, and shields. Shards of obsidian and rusty nails had turned his fingertips into ground beef after a mere hour of work, and thirst was an ever-present torment. Dust rimmed his eyelashes and clung to his hair. The fact that half of his face still ached from Leto's knuckles did not make him any more comfortable. Kaskil seemed particularly unhappy about their assignment.

"Leave it to Leto to give us the shittiest job in the Fort," he grumbled, "on the shittiest, hottest day of the year."

"Hye, you were the one who attacked him," Jack chuckled. "What'd you think was going to happen?"

"Please. I could tell *you* were *this* close to doing the same thing." A moment later, the head of his mallet slid off the handle and bounced off the back of his hand in mid-strike. He cursed loudly. "That's the fifth fucking time!"

"Try hammering less . . . angrily," Jack suggested with a smirk, brushing a long strand of gritty hair out of his face. He'd run all out of hair ties.

"Oh, cuz' I know you're just loving this." Kaskil stuck out his jaw. "Seriously, I don't know what's gotten into Leto. Just two days ago: 'oh, we're all great pals'; then yesterday: 'actually, go fuck yourselves'; then today: 'go do bitch work'. What a man. What a *loyal* friend."

"Speaking of bitch work," Flint said through clenched teeth, then sucked on an injured thumb. "Could you *stop* bitching? God, this is bad enough as it is without you running your fuckin' mouth."

Jack, in the middle of hammering together a shield, brought down his mallet and utterly disintegrated the target nail in red dust. "There goes another one," he said. "How many do we have left?"

Kaskil sucked his teeth. "Twenty? Thirty?"

"Any that aren't rusty?"

He gave a humorless laugh. Most of their nails had been repurposed from the hulks of old ships. "Good one." He sat silent for a moment, but couldn't for very long. "What is it, though? About them?"

Flint looked up, scowling. "About who?"

"The Outsiders? What's so special about them? Why do the Captain and Leto . . ." He searched for the right word. ". . . *worship* them?"

"I feel like that question's been asked before," said Jack.

"I know . . . but I don't get it. There must be *something*."

"Well, they're strong. They're helpful. Th–"

"Yeah, yeah, I've already gotten the fuckin' lecture."

Jack shrugged. "They don't eat or drink. Stopped doing it just to puke it all back up, too. They don't even pretend anymore. If they aren't wasting resources, I'd say that's in their favor."

Kaskil rolled his eyes. "Not that we know of. I mean, they aren't superhuman; that's impossible." He finished an arrow and tossed it into the pile. "But they're still creepy as hell."

Jack shrugged. "I don't like them as much as you don't, Kaskil. They're . . . strange. But the Captain and Leto clearly see differently, and I don't think we're going to change their minds anytime soon." Then, with some bitterness, he added, "Even though Leto's changed his own mind about three times on it."

"Well, they'd better start seeing our way. I mean it: something's gonna' happen. Something bad." He shook his head. "I just know it."

"Come on, Kaskil," Jack said with a roll of the eyes. "Enough."

"What, you don't agree?"

Jack just laughed and tossed aside a newly-constructed shield.

"But you said–"

"Yeah, I did. But I don't think they'll do anything to hurt us. I think we can count on that."

"Yeah?"

"Yeah. They just gimme the creeps, is all."

"That's all?" Kaskil said sarcastically. He scoffed.

Jack shrugged.

They worked in silence for a few minutes before Flint spoke up. "What do you think happened to the missing Outsiders?" he wondered aloud.

Kaskil smirked. "They aren't too good at keeping track of each other, are they?"

"Apparently not," Jack concurred, shattering another nail.

Flint raised an eyebrow. "What, are they infighting now? Leto's infectious."

Jack shook his head. "No. It's something else. Something . . ." He paused for a beat. "It's almost like they're–"

Presently, the sound of approaching footsteps made them turn their heads. It was Silas. He wore a bright smile, and looked fitter and healthier than any of them. He'd rolled up the sleeves of his plaid against the heat.

Jack tried to swallow, but his throat was dry.

"Hello, boys!" he greeted them, arms akimbo. "I see you're working hard."

"We sure are," Kaskil mumbled, only meeting his eyes for a moment.

"I'd just like to let you all know, and you especially, Jack, that we're all feeling quite at home with your tribe."

"Wonderful," Kaskil said, smiling forcibly. Flint looked away. "That's just *good* to hear."

"And we've decided to stay!"

Kaskil grinned wider. "Oh!"

"It was meant to be, really. Your people are so kind. Especially your chieftain."

"Yeah . . . he's a great guy. A really *great* guy."

"I'd just like to thank you all. Really."

"It's the *least* we can do." Kaskil kept smiling, but quivered a bit as he spoke.

There was a blank beat. Then, something occurred to Jack. "Um . . . Silas?" he asked.

Silas smiled. "Yes, Jack?"

"Well . . . remember when I told you — and it turned out to be a false alarm — that one of your group was missing?"

Silas furrowed his brow. "No, I don't, I'm afraid. But if you did, it was a terribly kind thing to do."

Jack stopped; looked at him. Silas stared back. Jack licked his lips and went on, deciding to ignore the Outsider's bizarre reply. "Thanks. But . . ." He cleared his throat. "See, last night I counted again. And I only counted seventeen."

"Yes?"

"So, I think somebody might be missing."

He smiled and shook his head. "I'm afraid you're mistaken. Thank you for your consideration — really. But I have the amount of people in my clan down pat. As you might have guessed, we've done a fair amount of wandering in these past few years, and I would *hope* I know the number of people I lead so as not to lose anybody. We're all very close, you know. And we've always had seventeen. Including myself, of course."

Jack cocked his head. A pang of unease rippled through his guts. "Oh– That's not what you said before. When I asked you, I mean."

"What'd I say before?"

"That you had *eighteen* in your clan, including yourself."

He chuckled in reply. "Well, I must have misspoke. How silly of me."

Jack looked at him. "Yeah . . . silly."

Silas slapped his sides. "Well, it was nice chatting with you three. Keep up the good work! It always gives me peace of mind to know you're out there every day, keeping us safe."

"We try our best," Kaskil replied dryly.

"You outdo yourself." He smiled warmly at them, then turned and walked away.

They sat in silence for a moment. Then, Jack exclaimed:

"That's it! I'm losing my mind!" He ran his hands through his dusty hair and shook his head.

"Did you see his arm?" Kaskil replied excitedly, smacking Jack on the shoulder repeatedly, eyes wide. "No wound! No scab! No scar! *Nothing!*"

Jack went silent and looked intently at Kaskil for a moment, trying to read his eyes, then smiled as if his shark-toothed friend was making a quip. But the air felt suddenly colder. Silas's sleeves *had* been rolled up, but Jack never thought to look for the spear injury that should have been there. "Funny, Kaskil. I can tell when you're joking." His tone suggested he believed otherwise.

Kaskil let his eyebrows sink. "Really? You think this is funny, Jack?"

"But . . . that's impossible! Come on, man."

"I saw what I saw."

"Well, *that's* fucked up," Flint said grimly, pinching the bridge of his nose. "That's *so* fucked up. First, they don't eat or drink, and now? Well, now . . . now . . ." He puffed out a breath through flared nostrils. "I'm getting too old for this shit."

Kaskil snorted. "What are you, thirty?"

"Shut up."

"This is ridiculous, you guys," Jack chided them. "Something's going on. I'll bet he was faking it yesterday. I'll bet it was deer blood on his arm, or something along those lines." He scoffed. "No way it was his. He probably just did it to seem all brave and heroic; make a good impression with our leaders. I'll bet that Bandit got in a fight with somebody else who wears plaid."

"Oh really?" Kaskil countered. "Why don't you go follow him back to his little pack of freaks and see for yourself? Huh? Go ahead."

Jack bit his lip. He had to do it. "Fine."

"Great. Or, you could just believe me."

"No," Jack replied, standing. "I'm gonna' show Leto. I'm gonna' change his mind."

"Best of luck," said Flint.

Kaskil saluted him. "Consider yourself witnessed."

Jack smiled despite himself, turned, and walked away towards the Outsiders' shelter. Only a few of them were there — but Silas was included. Jack walked perpendicular to them as if heading for the North gate, flicking his eyes towards Silas every few steps in as inconspicuous a manner as possible. Both of his forearms were a bit browned by dust and dirt, but the skin was, as Kaskil had said, totally undamaged. This was most bizarre. Jack turned and walked back, circling Silas. Silas, engaged in conversation with one of his followers, did not notice. From that angle Jack saw the same thing. Not a scratch.

One thing was clear — Silas hadn't been wounded. Jack was dumbfounded, but the truth was plain to see; Kaskil had not been lying. He felt relieved that Silas hadn't been the one to shred that unfortunate bandit. Just a single frame of the memory made Jack's stomach turn. He decided that he had seen enough and headed off to find Leto, uncaring whether or not his commander wanted to speak to him, and knowing full well that he himself did not really want to speak with Leto even though he had to. Leto's actions and words the previous day had stung, but Jack felt he had a duty to prove Silas's yellow-bellied doings. To open Leto's eyes. Somebody had to.

He found Leto sitting on his hammock, sharpening his knife on a whetstone. Leto looked up as he approached, tight-lipped. "Look who it is," he drawled. "You ready to treat your superiors with some respect?"

Jack raised his chin. "That's not why I'm here, Leto."

"Oh? Then why are you here, Jack? Because if I recall correctly, you and your unit were assigned a work detail this morning, and I want that work detail complete."

"Listen, Leto. I've got something important to tell you."

He scowled and continued sharpening his blade. "Make it quick."

"It's about Silas."

"Oh, God. Not this again. Didn't you learn your lesson?"

"Leto. It's his arm. There's no wound."

Leto barked out a sharp little laugh. "Sure, Jack. Get back to work and don't waste my time."

Jack sighed. "I'm not kidding, Leto."

"I'm at the end of my leash with your unit."

"I'll show you."

Leto looked up, his smile gone. "Really? You're serious?"

Jack nodded. "Follow me."

Leto hesitated for a moment, set down his knife and whetstone, and stood. "This'd better not be some bullshit prank. I hope you remembered the taste of my knuckles."

Jack ignored him. The anticipation of proving his commander wrong pulsed hot in his veins. But as they approached the Outsiders' shelter, he was disheartened to find Silas missing. He looked up and down the Fort but the haze of dust hampered his vision, and too many people were up and about. Leto stood next to him, arms crossed.

"Well?" he demanded. "Where is he?"

Jack ground his teeth. "I don't know, Leto. He was *just* here."

"I told you not to waste my time, Jack."

"Leto, I promise! If I could just show you his arm–"

"Hello again, Jack!"

He and Leto turned, and saw Silas. Jack looked down, expecting one thing but seeing quite another. Ice water flooded his veins. Silas's left forearm was bandaged and swollen, and very much indeed wounded. Jack, bewildered and open-mouthed, looked at Leto. Confusion swirling in Jack's mind. Leto narrowed his eyes at him. Jack could tell an inferno lay just behind those golden orbs, bottled up with a flimsy cork.

"Leto, I–" he began, but Leto cut him off.

"Silas," Leto spoke through his teeth. "Would you give us a moment alone?"

Silas nodded and walked off.

"Leto," Jack began in as subservient a tone as he could muster. "I swear, I–"

"Jack, just shut up."

Jack opened his mouth, then closed it. Leto looked at him, yellow eyes burning, then walked up so close to his face that Jack could feel his hot, putrid breath on his own cheeks. Leto spoke in a firm, measured tone, yet one that quavered ever so slightly like the slopes of a restless volcano. Tiny pinpricks of sweat glistened on his ebony skin. "Jack," he began. "I want you to listen to me *very* carefully. If you open that goddamn mouth of yours, I swear I'll give you a scar to remember it."

Jack set his jaw and listened.

"I want to make something *very* clear to you and to your unit, so I'd like it if you told them exactly what I'm about to tell you. Got it?"

Jack nodded.

"I don't know what it is that you, Kaskil, and Flint have got against Silas and his clan. What harm they could *possibly* do us is a complete fucking mystery to me. It's just *beyond* me how you could ever distrust them. Want to send them away. I can't understand it. But I know one thing." He held his finger up in Jack's face. "*I* was the one who made you a guardsman; *I* was the one who gave you that distinction; and the same goes for your friends. I'll bet you like being a guardsman, don't you?"

Jack nodded reluctantly.

"That's what I thought. Now, I want you to really take this in: just as easily as I put you three up where you are right now, I can take you right back down. Like *that*." He snapped his fingers. "So if I catch so much as a *breeze* of you three spreading any more rumors about them, showing them disrespect, trying to hurt them, *anything*, you'll be digging latrines and hauling water for the rest of your days. You got it?"

Jack swallowed. "Yeah," he muttered.

"That's *yes sir*."

"Yes." Jack ground his teeth together. "*Sir*."

Leto looked him in the eye a moment longer, his amber irises burning like twin suns, then slowly turned and sauntered away to the far side of the Fort without a single glance backwards, leaving Jack stunned and alone in the dust.

Jack did as Leto had told him. Kaskil and Flint were predictably enraged. The hammer of the former ended up lodged between two logs in the flank of the stockade. Leto was a bastard, they agreed. A tyrant. Then, after warning his comrades to lower their voices lest they be heard, Jack told them about Silas's arm, and they seemed about as unsurprised as he thought they would be, though he was still reeling in shock. To them, it was nothing new.

Leto kept them hard at work the rest of the afternoon, but they made the most of it. Any time their superior left the Fort or was out of sight, Flint would carry off one of two of the new weapons and stash them in an agreed-upon spot in the jungle, until they had amassed a small arsenal of spears, arrows, and bows. This, they all swore to one another, was to be kept strictly under wraps. And it was to be used only in the case of an emergency. If they should be split up at any time, the weapon cache was where they would meet.

Nothing made sense, but one thing was clear: something deeply unnatural was afoot.

Chapter Twelve

"Never thought I'd say this," Kaskil mused as they left the North Gate and headed back into the jungle, passing beneath the three bandits' decaying heads, "but I'd rather be out here than in there."

A patrol of the North Side composed their sentence of the morning. Leto had delivered this order as coldly and curtly to their unit as possible. Even maintaining a steely eye contact with his charges seemed to repulse him. His voice and manner was robotic, totally devoid of any emotion other than obvious contempt.

Jack didn't reply to Kaskil's quip, only marched ahead through the undergrowth. He was having trouble focusing on his fear of the jungle. Anger and confusion festered in his mind.

"He's a traitor," Flint growled. He led the trio, brandishing a machete against the attacking palm fronds. Jack could tell that he, too, usually just as perturbed by the forest, had his mind on other things. "A goddamn dirty traitor."

"Hey, you two!" Jack snapped, crushing a mosquito against the back of his neck. "Pipe down, will ya? Or we'll have company."

They got the message and walked on in silence.

An hour passed. Sweat trickled down the back of Jack's neck and beaded in his eyebrows. His hair was a ragged curtain spilling down the front of his face. Mosquito bites itched; burned; swelled. The early morning's rain still dripped down all around them though the skies were now plain and gray.

Kaskil was leading now. Jack walked behind him, and Flint brought up the van. It gave Jack an odd sense of Deja-vu.

THE JUNGLE NEVER SLEEPS

Ahead of them, the jungle began to open up. This area was known as the Thin Patch. Halfway between the Fortress and the foothills of the mountain, the trees began to grow further apart, the bushes fewer and less dense, and the steam thinned. Sunlight filtered through the canopy in shafts that grew wider and wider every few hundred paces.

Soon, the mountain was visible through gaps in the tree boughs ahead. When they reached the base of the foothills, their mission would end and they were to return home, but, oddly, Jack found himself savoring every step he took away from the Fort. Every moment that passed within range of an arrow, a spear, a poison dart was a moment spent away from the unsettling goings-on at home.

Ahead of them, the trail became very visible as the undergrowth thinned. Like a brown snake, it wound its languid way ahead of them through the ferns and creepers. It soon became obvious that it was impressed with fresh footprints. The sight of them made the hairs on the back of Jack's neck stand on end.

"It rained this morning," he spoke softly to Kaskil.

"Bandits," Kaskil affirmed, shifting his grip on his spear. "Keep your eyes peeled. Even in the thin patch, those bastards find ways to hide."

About ten paces up the trail, Jack noticed a number of palm fronds had been laid out across the path. The fresh footprints seemed to cluster around them. It struck Jack as funny. Why would the fronds fall so precisely? Why would the bandits take interest in them? Why had they gathered there? Kaskil did not seem to pay attention to this anomaly, and continued marching along. He stepped onto one of the fronds. His foot dropped straight down.

Jack lunged and grabbed Kaskil's arm, throwing his right foot out to brace himself as he heaved Kaskil backwards. Flint grabbed Jack around his midsection in turn. Kaskil teetered forward for a moment and cried out sharply in surprise — Flint and Jack strained in the opposite direction. Finally, Kaskil found his footing and stumbled away from the fronds, brandishing his spear.

"Jesus!" he gasped, turning his head this way and that, then down at the gaping pit standing before them. "What's that doing there?!"

Jack knelt beside the fronds, now partially bowing downwards into what appeared to be a sinkhole. He lifted one; tossed it aside. Then the next. Then the next. What he saw made his stomach turn.

"Damn," Kaskil breathed, his brilliantly blue eyes big as cannonballs. "It was almost lights out."

Before them lay a pit. It was a deep pit; nearly Jack's own height in its depth. And looming from the pit's shadows were the tips of a dozen sharpened stakes, like fangs in the mouth of some terrible beast.

It was no sinkhole.

"Shit," Flint muttered, shaking his head.

"This is fresh," Jack observed, prodding the loose soil around the edge of the pit. "Just dug, I mean. The dirt's not pitted by rain."

"It was dug after sunrise, then," said Kaskil. He lowered his eyebrows. "Hang on. If this was dug after it rained, then why are the stakes wet?"

Jack squinted. "I'll be damned."

Kaskil knelt before the edge of the pit and reached out towards one of the stakes.

"Careful," Jack warned him. "You're pretty heavy, you know. I bet you don't want me and Flint throwing out our backs trying to pull you out again."

The points of Kaskil's teeth flashed in a smirk. "Yeah, yeah. Quit bitchin.'" He extended a pair of sinewy fingers towards the nearest stake and rubbed his fingertips across its chiseled point; retracted them; licked them. Spat into the pit. "Poison. They've got poison smeared all over them."

"Poison?!" Jack exclaimed. "Jeez, someone wants us gone *bad*. You'd think the stakes alone would do the trick."

"Apparently not."

Jack crossed his arms. "Who'd do this? I mean, try to kill us?"

There was a pause. Jack could tell they were all thinking the same thing.

"Leto," Kaskil said bluntly.

Flint shook his head. "He can't possibly hate us that much."

"I don't know, Flint," Kaskil contested. "Haven't you seen him lately? He's not the man he used to be."

"How'd he get out here so fast?" Jack wondered. "I could have sworn I was awake before him."

"Well," Flint interjected. "One thing's for sure. This isn't the work of Bandits."

"How come?" Jack wondered.

"They aren't this *smart*," Flint conjectured. "Besides, they don't have the numbers, the cooperation, the time to pull something clever like this off. Always fighting each other. And the poison? *Pfft*. That's absurd. They're like animals; they're savage; they're moronic; the stakes would be enough in their minds. Or they'd just ambush us. If I was a bandit, I wouldn't go through all this trouble." He shifted his jaw. "Leto or not, someone in our tribe did this. Someone clever — not *too* clever, but clever enough."

"But *who*, if not our noble commander?" asked Kaskil with a smirk. He looked to Jack. "And how do you know it was *us* they were after, huh?"

"Because," replied Jack. "We were the first ones assigned to patrol this route today. The trap was meant for us."

Kaskil licked his lips in thought. "Do you think we should report it?"

Jack shrugged. "I mean, who's there to report to? The Captain?" He smirked. "*Leto?*"

"Jack's right," said Flint. "We oughtta' keep our mouths shut and our eyes open."

The three looked at each other, nodded, and headed back to the Fort.

Gene awaited them at the gate, leaning on his spear with eyes half-lidded. He was alone. Kaskil clapped him on the shoulder. "Guard duty as usual, eh Gene?"

Gene grimaced. "And second watch last night. I'm telling you, don't piss Leto off."

"What'd you do?" Jack inquired.

"Oh, well, I noticed the Outsiders still weren't eating. Or drinking. I was just worried about their kids, you know; so I told Leto to do somethin' about it." He chuckled. "I'm tellin' you, someone's got their panties in a bunch."

"Shocker," Kaskil grumbled.

"He backhanded me! — right across the face. See?" He pointed. The faintest trace of a bruise was visible. Jack felt his own mark of Leto's uncharacteristic fury. It still stung, but the swelling had gone down.

"It looks awful," Kaskil winced, trying not to smile. "Just awful."

"Thanks, Kaskil. Anyway, the bastard sent me out here on guard duty. Again."

"All by yourself, too."

"Yeah. Can you believe that?"

"Yes," said Flint.

"I'm sure."

"We got into a bit of a . . . scuffle with Leto yesterday," Flint continued.

"I was wondering how you got that, Jack," said Gene, pointing to Jack's bruise. "Your poor face, man. It's really been taking a beating lately."

Kaskil slapped Jack on the back. "Think of all the character you're building, buddy."

Jack smiled. "Think of all the ants I can shove down your boxers."

"What?"

"Oh, nothing."

"You won't believe what we ran into out on the North side this morning," said Kaskil excitedly. Flint elbowed him and glared. "Aw, come on, Flint. It's Gene."

Gene smiled. "It's me!"

Kaskil told him. He grimaced, sucked his teeth, and finally said, "Close one."

"Ha. You think?"

"Who d'you think did it?"

"We don't know," replied Jack.

"Bandits?"

"No, no, apparently they're too dumb." Flint nodded in concurrence. "We think it's someone from the Fort. Someone who knows we were the first unit to go out there this morning. Someone who wants us dead."

"*And* the dirt was fresh," added Kaskil.

Gene raised his eyebrows. "With all the drama circling the Outsiders, I'm not surprised. You guys talk to the other guardsmen much?"

Flint shook his head. Kaskil nodded. "Yeah. I mean, not too much recently. What're they saying?"

"It's weird. Some are suspicious of Silas and 'em all, but others defend them pretty adamantly. Like, won't hear anything against them. Especially Tom. There's been some pretty bad arguments." He exhaled. "I don't think they're dangerous. Just weird."

"Okay, enough," Kaskil spoke up. "You gonna' let us in, or what?"

"Oh, you guys want inside?" Gene chuckled. "You sure?"

"No, Gene," replied Kaskil. "We just *savor* every moment spent standing around out here wading through a fog of mosquitos while bloodthirsty hillbillies ogle us from the bushes. Could you move?"

Gene grinned and lifted his chin. "What's the password?"

"You're funny." Kaskil moved to shove past him.

Gene raised his spear. "Ah— What's the password? No password, no entry."

Kaskil sighed and crossed his arms. "Fine. How about . . . open . . . poppyseed?"

Gene ruminated on his words for a beat. "Close. You may enter." He opened the gates and swung them aside, bowing as they passed, and sticking out a leg to trip Kaskil as he did so. Kaskil kicked him in the shin as hard as he could.

Jack made a quick survey of the Fort's interior. Racks of fish were being hung to dry, and he noticed many of the Outsiders busy at this task. Still others were preoccupied with mending the stockade and hauling water. He tried to count them all, but found that it was an impossible task, despite the fact that the village seemed strangely empty. Silas was missing entirely. But Leto was not.

The moment he spotted their unit, a strange sort of spark flickered across the golden irises of his eyes. It was like the Green Flash seen so rarely at sunset — there one moment, gone the next, perhaps only a figment of the viewer's imagination. Jack could have missed it if he'd blinked. And there too, he swore, was the faint ripple of the Lead Guardsman's jaw muscles clenching the split second his gaze found them. Soon he was marching between the racks of fish jerky towards them.

Two men trailed close behind. They looked to be of Jack's age, both tall and lanky with too-big hands and sinewy necks. Their features were sharp, and their hair was bright red. They looked identical. Jack had never seen them before.

The South Gate was open behind them, and to Jack's surprise he noticed that a small dingy was being hauled up the beach by four of his fellow guardsmen.

Leto marched up to Jack's unit and stood before them, arms akimbo. "Jack. Kaskil. Flint." His eyes scanned the trio. "Any trouble out there?"

"None," Kaskil replied sharply. His gaze darted to the two strangers. "Who're they?"

Leto turned to the redheaded pair. He nodded to one of them, and said, "This is Lester." Then he nodded to the other. "And this is Caine. New guardsmen. They're . . . friends of Silas's."

"New guardsmen?" Kaskil replied, eyes narrowed. "What're you tryin' to do, replace us?"

Leto narrowed his own eyes. "Keep up that tone, and that's exactly what will happen."

"They fresh off the boat, or what?" Kaskil questioned.

Leto crossed his arms. "You got a problem with that, Kaskil?"

Kaskil opened his mouth but promptly closed it.

"Listen, Leto," Flint said. "What do we need 'em for? We've got plenty of guardsmen."

"*Protection*, Flint," Leto sneered. "Especially for Silas's people. You know they need it. It's our job to keep them from harm."

Flint scoffed quietly. Leto cast a withering glare in his direction. Lester and Caine simply stared at the trio, unblinkingly, and Jack's decision to meet their eyes was one he would regret. Their irises were completely white. A chill slithered down his spine.

"I see your attitudes haven't gotten any better." Leto crossed his arms. "Guard duty. All three of you. Rest of the afternoon. We'll see about the night."

Kaskil's jaw dropped. "We haven't done–"

Leto held up his finger. "Remember what I told Jack."

Jack felt a bubble of anger rising in his chest, but forced it down even though he could feel his veins physically itching. Kaskil gritted his teeth but said nothing. Flint was equally silent. Leto, looking pleased with himself, ushered them out through the gates and slammed the heavy wooden doors shut behind them.

"Look who's back!" Gene exclaimed. "What, Leto give you a hard time?"

"You could say that," Jack groused.

"What about?"

"Well," Flint began. "We've got some new friends."

"Who?"

"You'll see 'em for yourself," said Flint. "They're . . . creepy."

"Creepy as hell," Kaskil added. "Their eyes—"

"Did you hear what Leto said?" Jack interjected. "About them being guardsmen? They only just showed up, and already Leto's hired them on. I had to train *hard* before I got a spot."

Flint shook his head. "It's ridiculous. Leto, he . . ." He pinched the bridge of his nose, and said nothing else.

Kaskil grunted and kicked one of the doors, making it quiver and groan. "I don't know what's wrong with him! He acts like . . . like he runs the place!"

Gene looked at the ground. "Yeah. He's different now, isn't he?"

"Completely," said Jack.

"Weren't you guys friends with him before?"

"Great friends," Kaskil assured him. He shook his head. "It's wrong. Everything's wrong. There's something wrong with him, the captain, those goddamn Outsiders—"

"I think that's well established," said Flint.

"I've noticed something else," Gene spoke up.

"Yeah?" Jack asked. "What?"

"Is it just me . . . or, well . . ." He blew out a puff of air and slapped a mosquito against his arm. "Are there less of them now there are before? Of the Outsiders?"

"You noticed that, too?"

"I guess. But *are* there?"

Jack nodded. "Definitely. I've been counting them."

Gene raised his eyebrows. "Oh, you're serious about this."

He smirked. "Just curious, that's all. It's weird. Every day or so, one of them just vanishes. When I asked them about it, they denied it even though I think they'd all know each other pretty well. And yesterday, when they were down to seventeen, Silas denied it *again*."

Gene furrowed his brow. "That's..."

"...my thoughts exactly."

"Were they ever there at all? Maybe you were getting our people mixed up with theirs."

Jack considered this for a moment. "I don't know. Maybe."

"Nah," Gene reconsidered. "How about this: I'll bet they're starving, or dying of thirst."

"I think that's off the table," Flint said. "Since they got here, it's been way, way longer than somebody can survive without water. *Especially* water. Even without food, they'd already be too weak to work as hard as they do."

"Strange."

Jack nodded. "Strange."

"Hey," Kaskil spoke up, his tone lighter. "Why don't we play a game?"

Gene grinned. "How about..."

But Jack didn't hear what game Gene had to suggest. Something else intrigued him. He slipped back through the North Gate, unnoticed by his friends, and re-entered the Fort. His eyes searched for Caine and Lester. Spotted them with Leto. Shouldering past Outsiders and villagers, he snaked his way through the crowd and stopped twenty paces from where they stood alongside the South Gate. Jack pressed himself up against a sheet of metal siding acting as a barrier between two families' quarters. Leto said something in a low voice to his new charges, and they filed out of the gate behind him. Jack drew a deep breath and slunk to the gate, catching one panel before it could bang shut. He looked through. Nothing but beach and palm trees could be seen. He stuck his head all the way through and looked up and down the stockade just in time to see the trio vanish westwards around a corner. Jack squeezed through the panels and followed them.

When he reached the first corner, he flattened his back against the stockade and peered around it. Leto, Caine, and Lester stood huddled together not ten paces from where he stood, speaking quietly amongst one another. Jack swiftly pulled his head back around the corner and opened his ears.

"–some difficulties." That was Leto.

"Yes," said either Caine or Lester. His voice was unsettling crisp. "You requested assistance, sir. Silas sent us."

"And here we are," chuckled the other of the pair.

"I cannot express my gratitude. Was the journey hard?"

A sharp laugh. "Us mortals do not fare so well without food and water — unlike you, sir."

"But," said the other, "we are happy to serve Silas."

"We are risen," recited Leto.

"You are risen," the other two repeated, in unison. Jack cocked his head and listened harder, feeling a cold twinge in the pit of his stomach.

"Now," said Leto. "I'll make it brief. You know that it takes our kind some time to regain our strength before we are able to reproduce. Because of this, we have been able to take very few of them. And they possess fire. You must know the effects fire has on my kind."

One of them must have nodded, probably in a grim manner.

Leto went on. "These humans . . . they are becoming suspicious; they have started to notice something is amiss. Not all of us are good actors." Either Caine or Lester gave a small chuckle. "A few of the humans, too, have given me quite a bit of grief."

"So you want us to . . . eliminate them?"

"No," Leto replied. "I will take care of them. One is stronger, whom I hope I can take for myself, but the others will be disposed of accordingly."

"Why, then, did you call upon us?"

"Because," said Leto. "We are few, and we are still weak. You will help us ensure everything goes . . . according to his plan." He paused. "Do you understand?"

"Yes," Caine and Lester replied in unison. One of them then said, "Do not doubt our competence, sir. We are His loyal servants. We will assist you in carrying out his will to the best of our abilities."

"Many thanks, Caine. Many thanks, Lester. You may be mere mortals, but we and other factions of the Elevated cannot fulfill his vision alone." A beat. "Enough talk."

"Yes."

"Be gone. Speak not a word of this. We are risen."

"You are risen," said Caine and Lester in unison.

Jack heard footsteps approaching and sprinted away toward the South Gate. He slipped through and blended into the swarms of laboring villagers, his heart pounding in the back of his throat. He felt itchy; uneasy. None of it made any sense. He considered his options — should he tell the others what he had heard? Would they believe him? Did he know what he had heard at all?

In fact, he was having some difficulty remembering *anything* that had been said outside the fort. They had spoken so quietly.

Jack shook his head and rubbed his temples. It was nonsense. The Outsiders were probably just some kind of religious sect; after all, the Outsiders had reminded Jack of a cult all along, with Silas as their unnervingly charismatic frontman. That checked out. He decided to put it out of his mind. Leto had been speaking nonsense, and Jack was already certain that he was out to kill them all. From now on they'd be more careful. They'd sleep in shifts. Never go anywhere alone.

But he wouldn't tell the others what he had heard. Not now. Though some part of him begged the opposite, the other thought it strangely unwise. Perhaps that was self-detrimental. Perhaps not. None of them really knew anything about what was happening, so what was the point of sowing more fear? More confusion? All they could do was exercise caution. That and nothing more.

He returned to guard duty with his friends and spoke not a word of what he had passed between Leto and the newcomers.

Chapter Thirteen

They slept in shifts that night, but Leto made no moves to harm them, and the Fort remained dark and peaceful from sundown to sunup. Not a soul stirred. Still, Jack felt relieved when he opened his eyes and his soul still inhabited his skin. The early morning was clear and bright and warm. No rain had fallen during the night.

Jack sat up and stretched, feeling worn-out as ever. He ran his fingers through his hair. His scalp was greasy and itchy, and his arms were stained with dirt. It was high time that he went to the creek and bathed.

"Hey," Jack said to Flint and Kaskil, the former of whom was just stirring and the latter of whom had taken the last watch. "I'm gonna' go wash off in the creek, okay?"

They acknowledged this, and he stood before his way to the South Gate. There were very few souls up and about as the sun had not come up yet. However, he kept a wary eye out for Leto, not wanting to have his morning derailed into menial labor. Their paths did not cross. However, Jack made note of the Captain talking to a group of Outsiders outside his hut. Caine and Lester were among them. Jack put his head down and walked quickly past and out through the gate.

A cool breeze was blowing from out on the reef, where the *Luzon's* rusted skeleton was pounded by breakers. Jack stood outside the gate for a moment and let the breeze dance across his skin and through his hair. In the shallow lagoon between the reef and the shore, a small knot of villagers were hauling in their nets. Jack waved to them as he passed by on the way to the creek.

The creek was just to the west of camp. It was the source of all their fresh water, and was wonderfully cool. They weren't really supposed to bathe in it — even though the current flowed rather quickly — but Jack hated the crusty, salty texture of his skin after doing so in the Ocean. As long as Leto didn't spot him, he would be alright.

He eventually reached the place where the creek, after winding its tiring way down from the mountain and through the jungle, cut a deep furrow across the beach before spilling out into the sea. Jack followed this cut up to the edge of the forest and found where the well-worn trail of the water-bearers beckoned. After a quick look up and down the beach to make sure he wasn't being followed, Jack slipped into the jungle.

The trail led him to a low, muddy point in the riverbank that was impressed with countless footprints, and here he stripped off his clothing and waded into the current. It felt wonderfully soothing. He quickly washed off and was about to leave to the enticing waters and head back, but decided it couldn't hurt to stay in for a bit longer. He swam to the other bank and back a number of times, tried to see how long he could hold his breath, and got out on the far bank before swinging back into the water on a low-hanging vine like Tarzan. He felt like a child again.

But sooner or later, he knew his fun had to come to an end, for nowhere on the Island was really safe. Danger seemed to lurk behind every fern. It was sobering to think of as he climbed from the creek and dressed, his happy grin erased. He was reminded of visits to public pools that now felt so very long ago.

Still, it had been nice to pretend.

On the short trip back to the Fort, he decided to walk through the surf at the water's edge and look for whatever flotsam or jetsam might have washed up during the night; the Island's location in the center of a major current meant that curious treasures were always drifting ashore. Not much turned up by the time he had almost reached the Fort. He had so far spotted the husk of a cuttlefish — a novelty indeed, but nothing more, and certainly nothing manmade revealed itself in the froth and sand.

Then, just as he was about to call off his beachcombing, something caught his eye. It was black; something fabric. It almost looked like — ah, but was quickly sucked back out into the next wave. Not wanting to get his boots wet, Jack knelt in the wet sand and waited for the wave to return. It carried the strange object with it. Jack picked it up. He studied it for a moment, then smiled. It was the captain's cap. He'd been without it for days at that point, and Jack had been wondering whether the old man had lost track of his prized possession. He turned the cap around and around in his hands, and, sure enough, *"Luzon"* was emblazoned in gold lettering across its front.

But as Jack stared at the cap, he noticed something odd. He looked closer at the gold trimming and letters. They were stained — not by water, but by something that had taken root in the tightly-knit fabric and could not be washed out. The Captain always kept his uniform clean and wouldn't dare allow his cap to be blemished like that. Not only that, but the ruddy-brown color of the stains suggested only one thing to Jack.

And there was something else. The cap felt strangely heavy. Jack turned it over; looked inside. A strangled cry of disgust escaped his throat. He dropped the cap back into the water and started to back away, but his eyes quickly found something else that chilled him to his core.

A long, dark shape was drifting towards the beach, revealed in little glimpses at the crests of the waves that rolled in from the reef. Jack's mouth went dry. He knew what the dark thing was. Every part of him did.

Hesitating no longer, he turned and retreated quickly up the beach to the Fort, feeling as if something was chasing him all the way. The Captain's hat wallowed in the froth for a moment longer before it was drawn back out to sea, drawn back to its former owner, the currents unable to dislodge bits of bone and scalp still embedded in its lining.

Chapter Fourteen

When Jack burst through the South Gate, his eyes were searching for one thing and one thing only. They scanned the long-familiar faces of the villagers, the now-familiar ones of the Outsiders . . . and latched onto their target. Jack was dumbfounded. There stood the Captain exactly where he had been doing so before. It was him, in the flesh. There was not a question in Jack's mind about it.

But what had he seen at the water's edge? How could he explain it?

Just then, two of the Outsiders shoved past him and pushed through the gate in the opposite direction from which he had come, muttering something about him being in their way. They seemed to be in a hurry.

Jack ignored them and set about finding his friends. It was not a difficult task, as they were still in the process of eating breakfast along with most other inhabitants of the Fort, and he quickly made his way to them, shouldering past others standing in his way.

"Look who it is," Kaskil greeted him. "We were beginning to worry."

Jack had no time for niceties. He knelt beside them, and speaking in a voice both low and rife with urgency, said, "I saw something. Down by the water."

Flint raised an eyebrow. "Like what?" he asked.

Jack looked around. "Not here." He stood, beckoning. "Follow me."

Kaskil groaned and stood, but Flint, obviously curious, did so without complaint. Jack led them through the South Gate and halfway down the beach, but stopped there. Kaskil and Flint came to a halt beside him, their eyes searching the water. Jack advanced a few more steps but stopped again. Confusion swirled in his gaze.

"But . . ." he said, his voice trailing off. "It was just there."

"What was there?" said Flint, but Jack ignored him and jogged down to where the sand turned wet. He scanned the waves. Looked up and down the beach. The hat was gone. The body was gone. But something did remain. As Kaskil and Flint bombarded him with questions, he crouched in the sand and scrutinized its scuffed surface. Though they were partially washed away, drag marks led from the water's edge and continued up the beach, accompanied by footprints on either side. The drag marks were about as wide as a human. As for the prints, they were dug deeply into the sand, as if those who left it had been hauling something heavy. Something . . . waterlogged. Jack remembered the Outsiders that had passed him on his way into the Fort.

"They took the body," Jack muttered aloud.

"What?" said Kaskil, just as confused as he was. "Jack, what's going on? You gotta' tell us."

Jack stood and his eyes traced the furrows the body had made as it was hauled up the beach. Halfway up, the marks vanished as if the corpse had been picked up. He turned to the others. "When I was down here, earlier," he told them. "I saw a body. A body that looked just like the Captain. Just out there." He pointed. "And there was a Captain's Hat, just like the one Cap used to wear. It said 'Luzon' on it. It was bloodstained. And there was . . ." He hesitated. "There were bits of hair and bone stuck in the inside."

Kaskil and Flint stared at him for a moment. "But," Kaskil protested, "I just saw Cap. He's right inside the Fort."

"I know," Jack replied. "That's what doesn't make sense. And right as I was coming back in from the beach, two of the Outsiders went past me." He pointed to the marks in the sand. "Whoever that was that I saw, the Outsiders dragged their body out of the water and up the beach. I'll bet they were trying to hide it." He paused. "I bet they knew I saw it." Another pause. "But why?"

"It doesn't make any sense," Kaskil concurred.

"Could it have been somebody else?" Flint suggested. "Bodies wash up here all the time."

"But the hat," Jack replied. "It was *his* hat."

"Didn't you say–"

"Yeah. There were pieces of somebody's skull inside it even though he's clearly not wounded." He sighed and kicked the sand. "I don't get it. I just don't."

Kaskil nudged him and started towards the Fort. "Come on. Let's go get our orders from Leto. We shouldn't hang around here."

"Yeah," Flint agreed. "I've got a bad feelin' about all this."

The day was long and hot. Though their unit was spared the ordeal of a jungle patrol, Jack figured that one unsavory task had to be traded for another. He was right. They were put on sentry duty for the entire day.

When the sun at last began to sink into a violet sky, the shifts were changed and they were called back into the Fort. Jack was exhausted, thirsty, and achingly hungry.

"Mind if I eat with you guys?" Gene asked them.

"Sure," Jack told him with a smile.

"I hope it's not Venison again," Gene complained. "I can't take it any more."

Jack gulped, his mouth watering at the scent of roasting meat. He'd eat grass if given no other option. Two meals per day was not something he felt he'd ever get used to.

"Someone's feeling picky," Kaskil chuckled, elbowing Gene.

"I'm sick of it," Gene groaned.

"Well, more for me."

"Hey!"

"What? I thought you said you were sick of it."

"I am!"

"Well, if you want to go and dig out a paddy field, go right ahead."

They sat down on their hammocks and Flint set about lighting a fire in the firepit. The sky above had turned a deep violet with streaks of blue; to the east, it was like a great fire stretching across the horizon. Bats, swift and silent, wheeled overhead in pursuit of insects escaping the campfires' smoke. A gentle breeze was blowing outside the walls of the Fort, cavorting amidst the fronds of the palm trees. They swayed gently, silhouetted against the orange of the eastern sky, as if beckoning night to come.

"Cozy little corner of the Fort you got here," Gene said, looking around their shelter. He gestured upwards. "It's got a roof and everything."

"Where's the rest of your unit? Jack wondered. "Tom, and . . . oh, who's the other guy?"

"Aaron?" Gene replied. "You know, I don't talk to them much anymore. It's strange. They used to be pretty friendly. Now, all they do most of the time is stare at me. Just *stare*. It's creepy."

"I'm sorry," Jack said.

"It's alright. I was never too close with them. I don't think they trusted me much, on account of these." He gestured to his narrow eyes.

Kaskil snickered, and Jack elbowed him.

"Dammit," Flint murmured, his bulky form hunched over the firepit as he tried to coax a flame to life. "Why's the firewood all wet? And the ashes . . . they should be dry by now."

"There won't be any need for that," came a sudden voice from behind. They turned to look — it was Leto. He carried an armful of Yams, still smudged with earth, and passed them out. "It's our best harvest yet. Eat up. You're lucky I'm feeding you."

Jack said nothing, accepting his meal without making eye contact with Leto. He looked to Kaskil and turned the Yam over and over in his hands. It was heavy, and still warm from being cooked. He could almost picture the flavor. The richness. "Nice change of pace, right?"

Kaskil scowled. He scrutinized his yam. "I don't eat vegetables."

"It's not a vegetable."

"Oh, shut up, smartass."

Meanwhile, Gene wolfed his own yam down and wiped his mouth. "You're right, Jack! That was great. God, I haven't had anything but meat in an eternity." Then he looked at them for a moment as if expecting something.

"Yeah, yeah," Flint said with a smirk, handing Gene his yam. "Here."

"Take mine, too," added Kaskil. "I don't trust anything that asshole gives me. Not after this morning."

Jack felt a small twinge in his gut at Kaskil's words. His mouth watered at the thought of sinking his teeth into the yam's tender flesh. But the memory of those glistening stakes, the strange words spoken between Leto and his new charges, the Captain's hat . . . they came flooding back all at once. Jack stared at the yam for a long beat, licking his lips. He was starving. But the thoughts swirling around in his head were numbing his taste buds; sealing up his saliva glands one by one. Was it worth it?

Don't.

"Uh . . . I think I'll hold off," he decided with a heavy heart. But he didn't give his yam to Gene; simply set it aside.

"Really, it's a matter of principle for me," Kaskil explained. "I don't touch anything that comes from the dirt. It's not real food. Besides, how do you think I stay lookin' like this?" He flexed his bicep and Jack made a face. "You're just jealous."

"Keep telling yourself that."

"I'm serious, though. We're meant to be carnivores. If you wanna' survive in this world, you've gotta' kill or be killed. Like that old book — oh, what's it called?"

Jack thought for a moment. "The *Call of the Wild?*" he suggested.

"That one."

Jack smiled. "I didn't know you could read."

Kaskil rolled his eyes. "Thanks."

"Come to think of it, I haven't seen a book in years."

"Yeah, I–"

He was cut off by a strangled gasp from Gene's direction. The sound alone made his stomach sink like a casket into the grave.

No.

Gene's eyes were bulging from his head. His skin was blue. Sickly white froth spilled from between his lips. He crumpled to the ground and began to convulse violently, hands clawing at his throat as if it were squeezed by a noose, or by the iron grip of some invisible attacker. Jack, Flint, and Kaskil rushed to his side and knelt, calling for help, calling his name, but it was too late. The froth turned a deep crimson. His eyes rolled back in his head. His convulsions slowed; slowed; he twitched, then lay still, his agony terminated. Jack stared at his lifeless form in horror.

I'll take care of them, Leto had said. It was all coming back, now. Jack moaned in horror, knowing it was too late, wishing he could have remembered in time. Of course. The Yams. Why hadn't he stopped Kaskil and Flint?

"Gene!" Kaskil cried, shaking his arm. Gene did not budge. Already his eyes were turning cloudy, and his skin cold. "Somebody! *Help!*"

Flint bowed his head. He knew the truth. "It's no use, Kaskil."

"Oh, God!" Kaskil whimpered, jaw quivering.

"The yams," Flint muttered, lips unmoving. "Jesus, they were–"

"Poisoned," spoke Jack.

Kaskil grit his teeth. "*Leto*," he snarled.

Jack had no reply. His throat could not form words.

Kaskil beat the earth with his fist, tears welling up in his eyes. "That fucking *murderer!* I'll kill him! I'll kill him!"

"Bastard," Flint uttered simply, his features grave and shadowed. "That *bastard.*"

"*I'll do it!*" Kaskil screamed.

Jack watched as tears glistened in Kaskil's eyes. It occurred to Jack that he'd never seen the man cry before. Never.

But Jack couldn't find the will to. Couldn't feel. He could only look on, unspeaking, his chest a void so black and cold and empty that he couldn't feel his own heartbeat. His mouth was dry. And his skin was cold. So cold. Kaskil's cracking voice seemed to fade.

Red bubbles still leached from between Gene's lips.

By this point, a small semicircle of villagers had gathered around them, their faces stark masks of awe, hollow and open-mouthed; silent. None stooped to help. They all knew he was dead. Some cried. One vomited.

Some unseen hand was twisting a knife of ice into Jack's guts.

Kaskil suddenly leapt to his feet, face contorted in fury. He shoved the villagers aside and ran out into the center of the Fort, screaming for Leto to come out, to fight him. He ran up and down the length of the Fort, throat raw, brandishing a machete in his hand. The Outsiders looked on from their shelter in silence. Then, his quarry unfound, Kaskil marched to the North gate, slammed it open, and was gone.

The villagers began to speak. They asked for the Captain. For Leto. Neither were forthcoming. They asked what had happened. Nobody spoke, but some knew. Time ticked past. Jack's mouth was a desert.

To him, it seemed almost as soon as the villagers had gathered to gawk over Gene's corpse, they lost interest and began to disperse back to their own shelters and meals, muttering solemnly amongst themselves as they walked away. Only a sincere few remained. That was when Leto appeared.

When he saw Gene's body, their commander's features seemed to sink. He struggled for words. "My God!" he gasped. "Gene, he..." He looked up at Jack and Flint. "What happened?"

Still, Jack said nothing. But Flint, his face hard-lined in fury, stomped up to Leto and grasped him by the collar of his shirt. He towered over his commander.

"Leto," he growled, eyes narrowed and blazing. "I think you know *perfectly* well what happened."

"Get your goddamn hands off of me!" Leto snarled, kicking at Flint. But Flint held fast. "I don't know what you're talking about!"

"He was poisoned, Leto." Flint's tone was frighteningly calm and measured.

"That's ridiculous!"

"You tried to poison us."

"How *dare* you accuse me of–"

"And the pit, Leto? With the spikes? I assume that was your work as well."

Leto struggled to escape. "You insolent *fuck!*"

"Kaskil will have your hide dangling from the North Gate if he finds you, Leto." Flint grinned a twisted grin, raising the glinting blade of his bowie knife up for Leto to see. "That is, if I don't do the deed myself."

Then they were upon him. The two newcomers, Caine and Lester, grappled with Flint and managed to pry him free of their commander. They held Flint away from Leto as he kicked and shouted and strained at the Outsiders' steely grip. Their monochrome eyes were cold and unfeeling. Leto strode slowly up to Flint and stood so that their noses were nearly touching, and spat in his face.

"Murder, Flint?" he said. "You really want to accuse me of *murder?*"

Flint bared his teeth. "If I could get my hands on you, you bastard, I'd make–"

"Oh, Flint. I'm afraid you've crossed the final line." The corner of Leto's mouth turned up in a searing smirk. "I don't think removing you from the Guardsmen is quite enough." He considered for a moment. "I believe . . . a more severe punishment is in order."

Flint struggled hard against Caine and Lester's hold. His gaze bored into Leto's flesh. "You *bastard*. We were friends, Leto. Remember? Huh? *REMEMBER?!*"

Leto ignored him, drew his knife, and pointed it at Jack. Jack fell back onto the ground and held up his arm in defense. It was shaking. "As for you, Jack," he drawled, eyes narrowed. "Night watch. No relief." He stowed his knife. "And if you start feeling a little sleepy, well . . ." He smiled to Caine and Lester. ". . . just know our friends will be keeping an *eye* on you." The pair shared a glance, then grinned witheringly at him.

Jack clenched his teeth, rising to his feet. It was difficult to stand. His limbs were quivering with a strange mixture of fright and rage. "Let him go!" he cried to the Outsiders. His head snapped to Leto. "Leto! Tell them to let go! He didn't do—"

Leto laughed, cutting him off. "It's a little too late for that, Jack. But don't worry. I'll teach him to respect his superiors."

Help him.

"You wouldn't . . ." Jack spoke, voice quavering. "You wouldn't *kill* him." Jack knew, though, that every part of him, every cell in his body believed the opposite. He knew the truth. But Leto's answer was somehow far more chilling.

"Kill him?" he laughed, turning to Flint. "Oh, no! Oh, no no *no*. Unlike what you so desperately wish to believe, Flint, I'm not so base as to take the life of an innocent man." Then he grinned. "But when I'm done with you, you'll *wish* I was."

A glint of something flashed through Flint's eyes. It was fear. Jack started to feel the cold dissipating from his body; melting away like springtime ice. He felt his blood heating up. Anger was taking over.

Some part of his mind begged him to attack Leto, to free Flint, but he couldn't bring himself to move. "Please, Leto," he pleaded. "Let him go. Just let him go. You don't want to do this."

Leto lifted his chin, flexed his jaw, and turned to walk away. "Don't bother following us, Jack. I don't think you want to share in your friend's . . . education." He walked about ten paces, then turned, and said: "Oh, and, Jack?"

Take him down.

Jack gritted his teeth, hand itching at the hilt of his knife. He said nothing.

Leto smirked. "Good luck tonight," he said.

A chill ran down Jack's spine. He watched as Caine and Lester dragged Fint away, snarling and thrashing and kicking, and, led by their commander, they vanished through the South Gate. Jack was left in stunned silence. His blood stung in his veins. His eyes were locked on the doors of the Gate, still swinging from where they had passed through.

Go. Fight him.

His mind itched. It screamed. It begged. Begged for him to follow. But what would he really do? Fight Leto? It was laughable to think of. He barely noticed as Tom and Aaron, Gene's companions, returned from their watch. They barely gave the body of their old comrade a glance before moving on. The pair looked almost satisfied.

Then the doors of the Gate parted again, and through them strode Caine and Lester. They came to a halt before him, spears in hand, and glared down at Jack.

"Let's go," Caine commanded him with a sharp gesture of his pike. "No funny business."

Jack looked at the Outsider for a moment, his blood boiling. He gritted his teeth. Took a shaking breath. Nodded.

They led him at spearpoint to the ladder, and he climbed it to the top of the stockade.

Caine and Lester looked up at him for a beat, then turned and filed back out through the gates. Jack's conscience urged to climb back down the ladder. To follow them. To save Flint; to find Kaskil. But he couldn't do it. He couldn't.

Night fell, and he was alone again.

Chapter Fifteen

Jack paced back and forth along the catwalk. A sliver of moon cast its eerie light onto the scene below. The fires had been extinguished, voices had hushed, and now the only sounds were the chatter of frogs and the soft roar of the breakers far off in the distance.

Jack thought about what to do. What he *could* do. Kaskil was gone, but that meant he was safe. That gave Jack some peace of mind. Flint, though... his guts twisted each time he recalled Leto's words.

When I'm done with you, you'll wish I was.

He didn't dare deliberate over it. The meaning was clear enough. Thankfully, no screams had yet pierced the night.

Jack cursed his own actions. He felt like just as much of a traitor as Leto. He replayed the events that had gone down just minutes before over and over again, when he'd stood there like a spineless coward as Flint was hauled away. It had been betrayal; cold, hard betrayal. He wanted to punch himself straight in the gut. Wished he were in Flint's place. He kicked a support beam and grunted through his teeth. With each passing minute, he cared less and less about what might happen to himself and more about what might happen to Flint. His mind was eating itself from the inside out. Centipedes crawled under his skin.

Suddenly, he'd had enough. It was time to act. His comrades were counting on him, Flint especially, and to abandon them now was too great a betrayal for Jack to allow himself to live with. He'd done enough of that for one lifetime. But could he find Flint? Find Kaskil? Probably not. But he had to try. He had to take that chance. Because he knew, crystal-clear, that they would have done the same for him.

Eli's dog tags clinked softly together beneath his shirt, and the sound only fueled his fire.

For you.

It was decided. He would go.

He turned, spear gripped tightly, and began making his way towards the ladder. But he stopped. A darkened figure had reached the top of the ladder and was clambering atop the catwalk. They rose to full height and faced Jack. Details were hidden by the darkness, but whoever it was was tall. That could mean only one thing to Jack.

Caine began to advance, taking long, powerful strides. Jack felt a bolt of fear shoot through his nerves. He looked over the side of the catwalk — no, it was too high to jump. And the catwalk was no more than two feet wide. He bit his lip. Took a deep breath and steeled himself. He knew, deep down, that he would have to fight, and he would have to win if he ever wanted to see his comrades again. There was no other choice. He set his jaw, gripped his spear, and began marching towards his enemy.

He wished at that moment that he had a gun. But then he remembered what Kaskil had said: *Guns lie to you.* He hoped, unlike a bow ever did, that a spear would tell him the truth.

They were less than twenty feet apart when Caine made the first move, but Jack, seeing him raise his arm to throw, ducked just as the Outsider's spear shot over his head, whistling through his hair. He leapt to his feet immediately and threw his own spear. But Caine, in turn, dropped to one knee, and to Jack's astonishment, caught the weapon. He grinned, turning it around and facing it at Jack. His too-white eyes were visible in the darkness, their pupils like twin black holes. Then he sprang forward from his crouch, driving with the spear. Jack knew he could not duck in time. He twisted his upper body and stepped aside at the last moment with a grunt, heels teetering over open air, and felt the obsidian head of the spear slice a long, thin line through the stomach of his tank top, missing his skin by a hair's breadth. It was Jack's move. This was his window of opportunity — and it encompassed a split second.

Caine had been clumsy, and there was little room for error on the narrow catwalk. Expecting to run Jack through with his weapon, which he rightly should have, he put all his weight into the thrust and stumbled when his target evaded him. His target did not waste this chance. All at once, Jack lunged and shoved him over the edge of the catwalk. Caine didn't even have time to cry out or dodge the attack. His body fell like a sack of flour and landed with a dull crunch among the ferns.

Jack stood still for a moment, adrenaline pounding in his veins. He looked over the edge. Nothing moved in the foliage below. He exhaled in relief, surfing his heart rate as it slowly wound down, patting himself for injuries although there clearly were none.

The encounter had lasted barely a handful of seconds. He was surprised how easily Caine was beaten. But he knew he couldn't stand around in the open for long; there would be others that would come for him, and he had a mission. He turned back to the ladder.

Then came a sound. It was unmistakable, like a beating war drum — footsteps. His head spun towards the source.

Lester was approaching.

The Outsider took swift, broad strides as he approached, boards quivering beneath his feet, the blade of a knife glinting from his fist. He made not a sound. Jack drew his own knife and stood his ground. This was his fight to win.

Lester halted before him, knife raised. His irises and teeth gleamed white under the moon; his hair looked shockingly, strangely purple in appearance.

He feigned attack once, twice; grinning all the while. Then he struck out with his blade in a blur of motion. Jack blocked his move with one hand, then swung his other to strike Lester in his side with his own knife, but Lester dodged, wrenched his hand away, and swung his blade again. Jack leaned away hard, spine arched, as Lester's blade missed his chest by an inch. He stumbled but caught his footing. Feigned an attack on Lester's right. Lester moved his free hand to block, and, in the blink of an eye, Jack went for his left side. Lester spun away and grinned at him, crouched, swaying side to side. Jack took up a similar stance. He felt neither fear nor anger. He was immersed. Coldly determined. He *was* his blade.

Lester swung for him.

There was nowhere to go. Lester's blade arced towards his face. Jack jerked his head aside and the Outsider's knife hissed past his ear. Then, in a single motion, he crouched, reached up, grabbed Lester's outstretched arm and pulled Lester past him, using his opponent's momentum to make him stumble. Jack spun, rose, and drove his knife into his opponent's back before he could turn. Lester screamed and whipped around, slashing madly with his knife. He roared and rushed Jack, but Jack dropped to the catwalk planks. Lester stumbled over him as his strike missed. Jack turned again and kicked Lester's legs out from under him before scooting away and jumping to his feet. Lester did the same, wincing in pain. He was grinning.

He charged again, swinging for Jack. Jack grabbed his knife arm before the blade could bite into him and moved to kick him again, but Lester was equally quick. He grabbed Jack's foot and yanked it sharply up, throwing him onto his back. Lester dove towards him, knife raised, but Jack's boot met his face and snapped his head backwards. The Outsider yelped again and fell short of Jack, who scrambled to his feet and charged Lester. Lester rose to his knees, but was toppled to the planks, and then Jack was upon him.

The two grappled fiercely, slashing with their blades and kicking and punching and rolling back and forth on the narrow catwalk. All technique and fighting form was gone. It had been a battle to the death from the beginning, but now it more closely resembled one than ever. Jack struck again and again, the tip of his knife meeting wood more times than flesh as Lester whipped his head side to side. Blood streamed from the side of the man's neck and his temple where Jack's blade had nicked home. Lester's hand which held his knife was flattened firmly to the planks by Jack's free hand. Meanwhile, the Outsider's own free hand punched and clawed blindly, his nails raking Jack's skin when they met it. His teeth were bared; his eyes were wild; his breath was hot and livid.

Then a sudden burst of pain struck Jack like a freight train as Lester's knee came up into his groin. His concentration was broken just long enough for Lester to free his weapon and bring it streaking towards his enemy's side. Jack took notice at the last split second and sucked in his stomach, but it was too late. The edge of the Outsider's blade met flesh and tore through it, glanced off his rib, and splattered blood down the front of his tank top. Pain erupted. It was incredible, fiery, almost blinding. Jack cried out through gritted teeth, willing himself not to lose focus, and grabbed the bandit's knife before it could strike him again. Another flash of pain as it sliced into the meat of his palm, but the attack was blocked. The muscles in Jack's arm shook as he held the knife at bay, and pinned Lester's thrashing legs down with his feet. The Outsider's blade quivered not five inches from Jack's face. Then Lester's free fist came loose and met the side of his face, the same side that was still tender from Leto's earlier punch. Stars danced across his vision, and before he could do anything, Lester's boot was planted firmly against his chest. Lester kicked. Before he knew it, Jack was off his opponent and gasping for air on his back. He watched Lester get up through pulsating vision.

Jack was hurt, but so was the Outsider. And Jack knew the man was injured far worse than he. Jack rose to his feet. Blood ran hot and sticky from his slashed side. The wound screamed as if pierced by the stingers of a thousand wasps, but it only fueled his will to fight. Eli's dog tags clinked together under his shirt. Jack knew his brother had suffered more than he ever had. More than this. He'd been tortured by the Soviets; had more scar tissue than skin on his back. Jack's pain was nothing. He smiled as blood trickled from his hand and ribs. The Outsider wasn't smiling anymore. He looked angry.

Jack marched towards him, knife at the ready. The Outsider feigned left, and Jack sensed it; blocked to the right. But Lester swung his knife down instead, and across — straight for Jack's leg. He jumped back — again, too late. By the time he regained his footing a weeping line of red was scrawled across the front of his thigh. Yet another dazzling explosion of pain resulted, this one nearly worse than the first. A muffled grunt escaped the prison bars of his teeth. He limped away backwards, trying to gather himself, feeling his own hot blood running down beneath his trousers. The pain was inescapable. He drew a shaking breath as Lester advanced.

You can take it. This is nothing. He's hurting worse.

Lester was, indeed, beginning to flag. Jack could tell his movements were slower, clumsier, muddier. The wound to his back was taking its toll. He didn't bother feigning this time and went straight for Jack's throat. Jack's hand shot out and met his forearm, then wrenched it aside towards his free arm, exposing his unprotected flank. Jack's knife arced through the air, glinting with Lester's blood, and sunk deep between his ribs. Lester screamed and twisted away, tripping over himself. A rill of blood escaped the corner of his mouth. Jack smiled, shifted his grip, and charged. He toppled Lester to the ground; raised his knife, plunged it into Lester's shoulder. Lester writhed in agony. Jack pulled out his knife; raised it, struck again. This time it went clean through Lester's hand as he thrust it out it in a feeble attempt to avert his demise. Then, nearly in the same motion, he pulled the knife free and sliced clean through Lester's right wrist, the one which connected to his blade, and the man's knife clattered to the planks. The blood burned in Jack's veins. It boiled. Bloodlust was taking over; his killer instinct; his primal savagery. His grin was a jagged wound. He raised his knife, aiming for Lester's throat.

Then came a pain so horrendous that Jack's attack faltered and he crumpled to the deck of the Catwalk beside Lester with a red-hot wail, spine twisting, limbs shaking. The Outsider had dug his fingers into the cut on his side. Touched his ribs. The pain was unlike anything Jack had ever felt. And then, Lester was on top of him, the man's knife back in his hand. The catwalk was so narrow that Jack's entire left half was hanging out over empty space. And then he realized he was weaponless.

Lester plunged his knife down, and Jack blocked the attack with his unwounded hand. But his strength was failing. Slowly, shakingly, the knife traced its lazy path down towards Jack's throat. His arm was quivering violently. Lester's black-and-white eyes burned. His horrible grin was back. Jack summoned up all his strength. Pushed down all his pain. Lester was dying. If he could only...

He flicked his eyes to the side. Saw his knife. Remembered his fight with the bandit — he could reach his weapon then, and he'd reach it again.

His arm struck out. His fingers strained.

His other arm didn't have much fight left in it; the knife was now inches from his throat. Jack reached harder. He groaned through gritted teeth, gasping for air, grasping at nothing. Only blood and wooden planks met his fingers.

Then they touched the edge of something. Something sharp and hard and wet. He clawed desperately at it.

Lester's knife was three inches from his throat.

Two inches.

One.

Touching it. So cold and–

And suddenly, Jack was holding his own knife. He swung it with a snarl of exertion, the blade arcing upwards towards his enemy like a meteor, and plunged it deep into the muscles and sinews and veins and arteries of Lester's throat. Blood spurted out like water from a sprinkler. Lester shrieked, a horrible sound that was half-gasp and half-howl.

The Outsider's grip on his own knife faded, and the blade clinked to the ground next to Jack's face. Lester stared at him for a moment, eyes wide, his grin fading as suddenly as his strength, blood pooling behind his teeth and seeping out in long, sticky strands. Jack ripped out his knife. Blood fell upon his face like rain.

Jack looked into Lester's eyes. Their gaze was strangely hollow. Like those of the Bandit, the fight had left them. They were dead. Lester slumped to the side, his body limp, and in the blink of an eye he was gone over the side of the catwalk. The Outsider's body hit the ground with a sound more satisfying than anything Jack had ever heard.

Jack lay there for a moment on the bloodstained planks, still breathing hard, pain running rampant up and down his body as if he were on fire. But he was alive. And he was victorious. He rolled onto his stomach and then struggled to his feet, moaning and wincing. He tested his wounded leg. It hurt bad, but he could walk. He tore two strips of fabric from the bottom of his tank top, tying one around his middle, and one around his thigh. They soaked through immediately, but would have to do for now. He turned in the direction of the ladder and limped towards it, passing over droplets, strands, and pools of blood; some his own, and some not his own.

He knew where he would go. He knew where he would find Kaskil.

Chapter Fifteen

Flint awoke to a pounding headache. He opened his eyes, but could see only the bark of a tree trunk. A fire snickered somewhere behind him. He tried to move — couldn't. He was bound to the tree. He twisted his head to the side, looked down, and saw a bank of thick ropes around his waist. He cursed under his breath. The cloudy memory of Leto knocking him unconscious, and what happened before, began to come back in bits and pieces, a shattered mirror into the past. The mere thought of his commander set his mind ablaze with fury. He struggled against the ropes, but found that his hands, too, were bound together on the other side of the tree trunk. He could tell his knife had been taken, and he couldn't have reached it anyway. He cursed quietly and strained against the ropes again. They were strong and thick. Escape would not be easy.

"Look who finally woke up," Leto chuckled from behind him. "I got a nice little fire going while you were asleep."

Flint said nothing, only stared at the mottled browns and grays of the tree trunk with his jaw tightly clenched, still pulling on his constraints even though he knew the effort was useless. He was trapped. But hope wasn't lost; Kaskil was free; Kaskil would come for him. Hell, if Jack didn't get taken out he would go looking for him, too. Flint just had to wait them out.

Flint could hear a metallic clink as Leto removed his belt and gave a low chuckle. Flint craned his neck so hard it cramped, vying to look behind himself, but was unable to see his captor or what he was doing. Unbeknownst to him, Leto had knelt before the fire, and, smirking with satisfaction, held the belt buckle over the flickering red tongues of the flames. "I'm gonna' teach you a lesson about respect, Flint," he said. "Before I take your form as my own, I'm going to make you suffer. Apologize. Beg me to stop." He paused, smiling. "And then. . . Well, I think you know what has to happen then."

"Fuck you!" Flint snarled through his teeth. "You'll teach me shit! I'll die before I ever tell your coon ass I'm sorry!"

Leto laughed, harsh and grating. "We'll see about that, Flint."

"Wait until the Captain hears about this," Flint retorted.

"I think you'll find that the Captain won't be of much help to you, unfortunately. He and I. . . Well, let's just say you were right when you told me I seemed like a different man then I once was." He chuckled. "I apologize. We do our best to imitate those we inhabit. I may not have been . . . convincing enough. But nobody's perfect."

Flint opened his mouth; closed it. "The hell are you talkin' about?" he said, brow furrowed.

"Isn't it obvious, Flint? Come on, I know you're not as stupid as you look. Yes, I tried to kill you and your unit. Twice. Gene just got in the way. From the start, you and your friends presented a danger to my people; a danger that needed to be eliminated. I would have inhabited one of you from the start, then taken on the others to gain their forms as well, but I knew you three were crafty. The other two would have become suspicious right away. And you were suspicious enough as it was. You were a threat."

"*What* are you—"

"Though we have now gathered sufficient strength to start multiplying, it was a risk I was not willing to take. So I tried to kill all three of you at once." He sighed. "As you can see, I did not succeed. But, tonight, I have all three of you in my pocket!" He smiled triumphantly. "Caine and Lester will take down Jack, and I've sent a little something *special* after Kaskil. Those two have to go, I'm afraid. My kind can only absorb so many forms. But as for you. . . Well, your physical form is much more desirable. So strong. So . . . robust. Really, I was planning on taking you all along when Silas just wanted you dead. It's a good thing for the both of us that you gave that yam to Gene. Once I get my apology, we will become *one*."

At first, Flint was at a loss for words as he, incredulous, tried to process what he had been told and convert it into something that made logical sense. The Outsiders had displayed... *unnatural* characteristics, but this seemed to be on a different level of unnatural. This was nonsense. Flint cocked his head, slack-jawed and smiling, and said, "You've lost it, haven't you? You're crazy."

Leto laughed good-naturedly. "I guarantee you that I am, in fact, *not* insane. But if I do not consume a new manifestation soon, I will grow... quite irritable. So let's crack on, shall we?"

"You're a lunatic," Flint said, shaking his head.

Flint ignored him. "You can give me my apology the easy way, or the hard way. It's up to you. Either way, that skin of yours will be mine in the end."

Flint laughed aloud. "You're out of your goddamn mind, Leto. You're sick."

"Ah. The hard way."

Flint scoffed. "You think you can break me?"

Leto removed the belt buckle from the flames. It was glowing yellow. "Yes, in fact. I think I can. But don't worry. We'll start small." He gave the belt a couple of twirls. It felt good in his hands. "Now, all I need you to do is apologize for disrespecting your superior. Got it? Apologize, and we're done. Our forms can finally merge."

Flint laughed out loud. "Disrespectful? Oh, that's rich."

"How's *this* for rich?"

A crack resounded, and the belt buckle sliced a long, red, arc of sizzling flesh down Flint's back. A strangled snarl escaped his throat. The pain was unlike anything he had ever felt – white hot, searing, pulsating. And it didn't fade. He writhed against the tree, wondering, despite himself, how many more lashes he could really take. It was horrible.

Another crack, another slash, but this time Flint managed to keep silent, though his face shook and grew red as the belt buckle was. It hurt worse than anything he had ever felt. Worse than being shot. He could smell his flesh burning, actually *burning*, and a bolt of panic struck him, though he tried to bite it back. His friends would come. They would come. He could hold out until then. He set his jaw and braced for the next blow.

"You ready to apologize, Flint?" Leto barked. "Huh? We could keep going all night. Those wounds don't bleed, you know. I could whip you to the bone if I wanted to."

"Go ahead and try," Flint gritted out.

Leto shrugged. "Have it your way."

He whipped Flint for a third time. Somehow, it felt indescribably worse than the two blows that had come before, and his spine arched as a million white-hot nails were driven into his twitching, bubbling flesh. It was horrendous. Flint took a deep breath and tried to steady himself, to sink into his imagination as he had done so often during the war; escape the harsh realities of the world and go someplace else, but simply could not. The pain was all-consuming. He wanted to escape not just his own mind but his own flesh; to crawl out of it and be free of that horrible pain.

Then he remembered something.

His wristblade.

He could sense it; still there, still lashed to his forearm, the little leather loops still wound around his fingers, ready to be pulled to extend the blade. He smiled through the pain. Hope sparked in his chest. He didn't need Jack or Kaskil. He could get out. He could do it himself. And then, he would give Leto a taste of his own medicine. He squeezed his fist shut, the leashes connected to his knuckles pulled, the blade slid from its scabbard onto the back of his hand. It felt secure.

He twisted his wrist and began, quickly and quietly, to saw at the ropes binding his hands. He prayed the blade was still sharp.

He could hear the whistle of the belt through the air as Leto wound up for another lash. It struck him. His eyes bulged from his sockets and air hissed between his teeth. He sawed faster. The first rope gave way as Leto wound up a fifth time. *Crack.* A brilliant explosion of pain, like fireworks under his skin. The acrid smell of burning flesh filled the air.

Focus.

The second rope binding his hands fell away, and now they were free. When Leto struck him a sixth time, he allowed himself to cry out so as to distract his punisher from what he was doing. Four ropes bound his waist. He began sawing through the first one.

Crack.

He squeezed his eyes shut and kept cutting, holding the first rope in place with his left forearm before it could crumple and give him away. Soon he was halfway through the second rope. But then, feeling about behind the tree trunk, he found something much more useful. The knot. Just as Leto recoiled to strike him a seventh time, he gathered all his strength, sliced through it, spun, and caught the belt buckle mere inches from biting into his face. It seared his palm, but he barely felt it. The look in Leto's eyes was simply too satisfying to bear. Joy rippled through Flint like the touch of sunlight after a long, cold night in the Cascades. There was a sinking of his commander's features, a flash of panic in his golden irises. Flint towered over him, leering down at his commander, his teeth bared in a twisted grin. He yanked the belt out of Leto's hands.

Leto began to back away, his hands held up in front of him. He was acutely aware of the fire flickering mere feet from where he stood. "Flint . . ." he began in a measured tone. "Don't do something you might regret."

"Regret? Ha! You're a murderer, Leto. A maniac. You're out of your mind." He flicked his eyes to the fire and stepped closer to Leto, who kept backing away. "I'll enjoy this."

"Join me, Flint," Leto begged, still shielding his face. "Let me take on your magnificent form, your– your *beautiful* form . . . let me inhabit you! I can make you immortal! I–"

It was too late for his pleas. Flint tackled him to the ground and twisted his arms behind his back as if he were a pretzel, and though Leto struggled with all his might, the huge man's grip was like titanium. It was inescapable. Flint held him easily as he screamed. With one knee rammed into Leto's back, Flint took a handful of the commander's hair and held his face just over the fire, letting the flames dance just past the tip of his nose and reflect, mirrorlike, against the sheen of sweat coating his chocolate skin.

"Please!" Leto shrieked, thrashing and bucking and kicking in a desperate bid to escape. *"No! Flint! Think of what we could become together!"*

Flint was practically trembling with excitement. He didn't bother holding back his grin. The pain in his wounds was all but forgotten. "Listen, Leto," he teased. "It's simple. All you've got to do is apologize and you can go the easy way."

"I'm sorry! Please! I can make you great! We *can–"*

Flint laughed. "What was that, boy? Speak up when answering your commander!"

"I'M SORRY! SPARE ME!"

"Speak up, private!"

Leto's vocal cords sounded as if they had been run through a cheese grater. *"I'M SORRY, FLINT, PLEASE!"*

Flint tsk-ed. "Too little, too late, old friend. 'Fraid you've crossed the line."

Then, with flames dancing in his eyes, he shoved Leto's face into the fire.

Chapter Eighteen

The frogs, the insects, the night-birds — they taunted Kaskil. He'd already circled the Fort twice, screaming the name of his commander until his voice grew hoarse, and then, assuming that cowardice had driven him into the jungle, Kaskil struck out into it. Trails eluded him, but he did not require their service. He plowed on through the undergrowth with a machete in one hand, slashing at ferns and creepers, channeling his rage into their destruction. A fire burned within him. Not all of it represented his anger at Leto; no, some of it was the agony of guilt. After all, he'd given his own yam to Gene. He'd passed on his death sentence.

An hour passed. The air cooled, but remained humid. Kaskil came upon a trail, and followed it away from the mountain. Perhaps Leto had returned to the Fort. Kaskil fantasized about what he would do when he caught up to his commander. It put a ghoulish smile on his face. The urge to avenge was the strongest urge of all. It was an itch; an itch deep within; an itch inside his bones, his muscles, the gray matter of his brain — and it needed to be scratched.

Then, he remembered the weapon cache. It was there that he, Jack, and Flint had agreed to meet if they were to be separated, and he assumed that they, too, recalled the pact. He carried only a machete at the moment. Not only he, but all of them, would need heavier armament in the foreseeable future. It would not be easy to find the cache with so little moonlight, but he would have to try.

Suddenly he found himself sprawled out on the trail, the toe of his boot still caught on an exposed root. He grunted and cursed and extricated himself, then stood. Stopped for a moment and listened.

A twig snapped.

Then another.

Kaskil's head swiveled, his blue eyes luminous in the darkness. He raised his machete and pressed into the undergrowth in the direction of the sound. It could be a bandit. But then again, it also could have been Leto. He wasn't willing to waste such an opportunity. He stopped; listened. There came a rustling of dead leaves from the undergrowth just ahead of him. Knuckles quivering at the hilt of his machete, he squinted into the darkness. Though his eyes had long adjusted to the midnight gloom of the jungle, very little light filtered through the thick canopy above and rendered the world below dim and murky even on the brightest of days. But as he looked, his eyes snagged on something.

It was a pair of eyes. They were yellow as Leto's, and for a moment his veins prickled with adrenaline at the thought of exacting his revenge, but a split second later he noticed something odd about the eyes. They had long, thin pupils like a cat.

A cat. It's just a cat.

His shoulders relaxed. The creature was probably a Wildcat. Leaves rustled as it slunk towards him through the undergrowth. Kaskil, without taking his gaze from the shadow-bathed beast, began to back away, careful not to trip over any more roots. He was unafraid. Wildcats on the island were rare, and normally quite small — unlike this one. But Kaskil knew he could take it on if he had to. A few weak shafts of moonlight played upon the creature as it emerged from the greenery, illuminating its mottled fur, rippling flanks, glistening fangs . .

Kaskil suddenly felt cold. The heat of anger and adrenaline slipped away like a winter sunset. Something was wrong. As the Wildcat approached him, one sinuous step at a time, it became clearer and clearer that this was no ordinary Wildcat. And it had been crouching. It drew within a mere ten paces of Kaskil before lifting its monstrous head and rising to its full height.

It towered over Kaskil.

My god.

Kaskil's jaw dropped and he found himself frozen, staring, unable to move. His knuckles were white around the hilt of his machete.

The animal was utterly titanic. It stood a full head above Kaskil. Its skull was like a boulder, with those terrible yellow eyes glowing out of it like twin lanterns, and enormous, dripping fangs like sabers jutting down on either side of its lower jaw. The gape of its mouth was unnervingly wide, with its corners nearly at the creature's ears, and rows of jagged teeth protruding between lips slathered in froth. Four legs like tree trunks supported its hulking body. Muscles writed beneath their spotted fur. Along its back, long, pointed spikes of bone protruded spearlike from its bony spine. They quivered as the Wildcat crept along. It licked its lips, and Kaskil felt a chill run up his spine. His legs started working again.

"G–good kitty," he groveled, backing away with his weapon held in front of himself.

The Wildcat gave a low growl, ears flattened, and its spines rose like hackles. It advanced on him. He backed away. Then, without warning, his back was pressed against the trunk of a tree. The Wildcat kept coming. Kaskil let out a small whimper. For the first time in as long as he could remember, real, unadulterated terror coursed through his veins. He knew he couldn't run from the beast. He would have to try and fight.

The Wildcat bared its horrible bank of teeth and settled on its haunches. Kaskil squared his own shoulders and set his jaw. He drew a deep breath. "Come and get me," he taunted, grinning, burying his fear.

I can take him.

The Wildcat sprung. Kaskil dove aside, rolled, and sprung to his feet, laughing. The Wildcat's fangs were embedded into the tree.

"Oh, I'm terrified!" Kaskil laughed. "I'm shakin' in my boots!"

The beast struggled for a moment, snarling, before it managed to pry its teeth free and throw itself at Kaskil once again. Kaskil anticipated its movements and rolled to the side again. It went crashing past him into a clump of ferns. He was sure the Wildcat could crush his skull like a cantaloupe, but it was simply too large to catch him. Kaskil would hold it off until his window of opportunity came. It spun and leapt again. Kaskil dodged. But this time, he was too late. At the last moment, the Wildcat sprung against a nearby tree and launched itself at him, knocking him to the ground. Kaskil yelped as he looked up into the creature's glowing yellow orbs. Drool dripped down onto his face. The beast's gigantic paws pinned him by the shoulders as easily as if he were a butterfly. It snarled, spraying him with saliva. He tried to kick, tried to punch, but his hands and feet were pinned. The creature lowered its muzzle towards his face, jaws agape. There was no escape. It was over. Kaskil closed his eyes and steeled himself for the end.

I've had a good run.

Then there came a dull, wet *thud*. Kaskil opened his eyes.

The Wildcat had frozen. Its eyes were wide with shock. Through the center of its skull ran a spear, the weapon's head dripping with brains. Slowly, shakingly, the beast turned its head in the direction of the attack, and it was then that a second spear cleanly pierced its neck. The creature wobbled drunkenly for a moment, then crumpled sideways into the foliage. It didn't move.

Kaskil laid there for a moment in the mud, his head racing so fast it felt as if it might burst. His hands ran shakily over his body, checking for injuries, but he doubted he'd be able to feel them in his present state. A question burned in his mind: who had thrown the spears? Who had saved him?

His question was answered when a shadowy figure stepped out from the undergrowth. It stood over him, silhouetted by a shaft of moonlight. Before Kaskil's fight-or-flight response could kick in, before he could grasp for his weapon, the figure offered a hand. Kaskil froze for a moment. Then he reached up and took it. The stranger pulled him to his feet. Once standing, Kaskil found it difficult to remain so. Adrenaline sped through his veins, making him feel numb and dizzy and giddy, but he felt a bit steadier once the moonlight lit up his rescuer's face. He looked at Jack and grinned.

"Doctor Livingstone, I presume?" said Jack.

Chapter Nineteen

Kaskil grinned wearily and hugged him. "Damn, Jack," he panted, shaking his head. "That was close."

"What was that thing?" Jack replied.

"No clue. It was *big*."

"At least it's dead now."

As if on cue, they both turned and looked at where the corpse of the Wildcat had fallen. But it was gone. Only a pool of deep-red blood marked the spot where the monster took its final breath. Kaskil shook his head in disbelief, unable to find the words.

Jack limped up alongside him and looked down into the mud and leaves. "Where'd it go?" he questioned, brow furrowed. "I just . . ."

"It couldn't have — no, that's not possible." Kaskil looked at him. "Nothing could have survived that, right?"

"Nothing."

Kaskil squinted into the darkness, then knelt. "Wait a minute." He inspected the mud carefully, then looked up at Jack, and said: "There's footprints here. Human footprints."

Jack felt a twinge of unease, but there were more pressing matters. He began backing away and beckoning to his friend. "Come on, Kaskil, we gotta' move. Leto's got Flint. If we go now, we might be able to find them before it's too late."

Kaskil bared his teeth and stood. "That fuckin' bastard."

"You got a weapon?"

Kaskil looked around for his machete, but it was gone. "Shit . . ."

"Here," Jack said, tossing him a spear from the bundle he carried under one arm. "I emptied out the cache. Let's go."

They bushwhacked a short distance before coming upon a trail and following it towards the Fort. As they ran along the path, Kaskil noticed that Jack was limping. "Whoah, you're bleeding!" Kaskil exclaimed, though he seemed less concerned and more enamored. "What happened?"

"Caine and Lester happened," said Jack.

Kaskil grinned. "Wasted 'em?"

Jack nodded grimly. Every step he took sent a screwdriver of pain twisting into the meat of his leg. "Both of 'em."

"Damn! That's hardcore!" He slapped Jack on the back so hard that Jack stumbled; nearly fell. He caught his footing and kept running with a loud wince. "You good?"

"I'm good."

"Lemme' guess, this was all Leto's doing?"

Jack grimaced. "You guessed it. Our courageous leader sicced them on me."

"Well, he should'a sent someone better!"

Jack just smiled a bit.

Kaskil laughed loudly. "Fuck, man, you're legendary! Two at once? You're a– you're a *machine!*"

Jack shrugged, and regretted it as his cut across his ribs was reopened. "I mean, *you* trained me, a–"

"No, really. You're makin' me all jealous. God, you have no idea what I would give to get my hands on that slimy little snake. I'm gonna' fuckin' skin him. No– it'll be worse than that."

Jack knew Kaskil was a man of his word, which was a bit frightening. His only reply was a brief nod and a single word: "Yeah."

There was a brief period of silence filled only by their muffled footfalls and the hiss of grasping vegetation as it brushed against their bodies.

"How'd you even find me?" Kaskil panted at length.

Jack grunted. "It wasn't hard. The two of you were making a racket back there. Besides, you weren't far from the Fort."

"Good thing you remembered our cache, too. I thought I was done for!" He laughed. "Shit, Jack, this is the second time you've saved my ass!"

Jack smirked. "You owe me."

"Damn right."

They reached the Fort in little time. Two guards who were posted outside the North Gate moved to stop them, but they shoved past and ran on along the fort wall towards the South Gate. From there, they angled off down another trail, this one being the path Jack had seen Flint dragged away down. They were enveloped by the suffocating greenery once again. Jack and Kaskil stopped talking at this point. Once out of sight of the guards, Jack stashed their bundle of weapons near a lightning-scorched tree stump. Then they moved along down the trail in silence, weapons in hand. Jack carried a spear. Kaskil; a bow.

The pair didn't have to trek very far. Jack figured they'd only gone a quarter of a mile before the stark yellow glow of a campfire beckoned to them from the darkness. They slowed, crouched, and crept along towards the flickering light. It was like a tiny sun in the darkness, silhouetting creepers and vines and ferns like shadow puppets.

Suddenly, as they drew near, a scream pierced the night. Jack's heart leapt to his mouth. Kaskil cursed. They came within ten paces of the fire and crouched behind a rotting log, then peered over it into the clearing, towards the source of the cries. Two figures were outlined before the flames. One knelt atop the other, holding their head just over the flames. There came another scream. It was a hellish daisy chain of unintelligible shrieking. But, although what was said was unclear, Jack could tell one thing right from the start.

Kaskil, nostrils flaring, nocked an arrow and drew back the string, aiming straight for the kneeling man. Jack clamped a quick hand onto his shoulder. "Kaskil, no!" he hissed. "Don't shoot! It's Flint!"

Kaskil lowered the bow and squinted. He smiled with satisfaction as the realization dawned on him. "I knew it. That bastard." He shook his head.

Just then, Flint plunged Leto's face into the fire. An unearthly wail erupted from the sizzling embers. Leto's body thrashed as if overcome by a seizure, his limbs convulsing violently, furiously, and, as Jack and Kaskil watched in awe, his entire body burst into flame. It was like he'd been smeared with gasoline. His limbs flailed wildly. The screams were horrible.

That was not all.

As Jack stared on, something unsettling happened to Leto's blazing form. He couldn't be sure what he was seeing, but as he watched, the body of his former commander seemed to *change* in the flames. To grow. Not only larger, but to grow . . . *stranger*. There was something about it he couldn't make out; something he couldn't admit even to his own mind, and just as it seemed his widened eyes were beginning to get a grip on what they were seeing, a sudden, blood-red geyser of fire shot up from the body, pulverizing it into ash, roaring and whistling, then faded. Flint cried out and stumbled away backwards.

"Flint!" Jack called, and stood. Kaskil did the same. They strode into the clearing and surveyed the scene. Leto's body was already a mere pile of ash, barely recognizable as a human. Around a nearby tree trunk, ropes were coiled. In the center of the clearing stood Flint. His shirt was in tatters, and pain could be read in his taut features.

Flint struggled to his feet and managed a weak smile. "Well, well, well," he drawled. "I thought chivalry was dead."

Kaskil laughed and moved to embrace him. "Come 'ere, you big buffoon."

Flint quickly backed away, trembling a little as he raised his hands. "Hey, um . . . I need you two to look at something." He looked ill at ease. "It's my back." He turned around, displaying his injuries. The broad landscape of rippling muscle was crisscrossed by blistered, fire-red strips of burned flesh. "Is it bad?"

Kaskil's eyes went wide. "Shit. That's gnarly."

"We have to get you to a hospital!" Jack blurted, then turned his eyes to the ground in embarrassment.

Flint exhaled sharply. "Thank you two for those words of comfort."

Jack's wounds suddenly felt a lot less painful. "Flint, your back is–"

"Yeah, I've heard enough. Charcoal here–" he gestured to Leto, wincing as he did so, "–gave me the belt. The metal end. It was heated up."

Jack scoffed. "Heated up? It must've been molten!"

"Tell ya', it felt like it." He looked at Jack. "Looks like you got into a little scrape yourself."

Jack told him what had happened. Flint raised his eyebrows.

"I'm impressed, Jack. Really impressed." He grinned through his pain. "Maybe a little scared."

Jack smiled and nodded his thanks.

Kaskil kicked the mound of ashes that had once been their commander. "Look at you, Flint, stealing my thunder." He tsk-ed. "I had an arrow picked out just for 'im."

"Yeah, and you almost got to use it," Jack said sardonically.

Kaskil elbowed him right in his injury. "Fuck off."

"Hey," Flint spoke up. "You two – we gotta' get out of here. Now. Did either of you clean out the cache?"

Jack nodded. "Yeah. I re-hid it, too."

"Good. I've got a feeling we might need to use it."

"I'm guessing going back to the Fort isn't an option," Kaskil grunted.

"You'd be right. Before he laid into me, Leto told me some absolutely insane shit. About the Outsiders. About himself. About the Captain." He shook his head. "It was crazy."

"What'd he say?" Jack asked.

Flint's eyes skittered to the side, as if expecting somebody to come darting out of the bushes towards them, spear in hand. "Not here. Not now. They'll be coming for us." He looked back at them. "We gotta' leave."

"Where do we go?" replied Kaskil.

Flint sighed. "Anywhere but the Fort."

Chapter Twenty

It was midday. The sun shined, and clouds scudded across the ocean of blue above like clipper ships. Jack looked out over his own sea and watched the waves roll in. He let his eyes unfocus; relax on the wind-rippled turquoise waters and the long, thin stripes of cottony white foam that cut through them. Palm fronds danced at the edges of the scene like a verdant picture frame. Amongst them, songbirds whistled and chirped.

He felt nothing but the kiss of the breeze and the sting of his cuts. He had killed; killed twice, and yet there was no feeling, no emotion. There *had* been emotion, of course, but it had outlasted its welcome quickly. He had not pushed it down but simply hurried it on its way. It had passed over him and through him and out of him as easily as the wind lifted a strand of hair, dropped it, and was gone.

As Jack gazed out over the waves, a funny thought crossed his mind.

This could have been somebody's vacation.

It very well could have been. And, he figured, in any other world, it certainly would have been his. He pictured himself kicking back on a padded deckchair, perhaps watching bronzed young ladies strut past in their bikinis. He could hear the faint screech of a Pan Am jet in the distance. The *tweet* of a lifeguard's whistle. He would have had an umbrella drink fogging up in his hand. Perched on the bridge of his nose, a pair of ray-bans may have rested.

Instead, there was a spear in his hand, and the bridge of his nose was tender with bruises. There were no girls. No jet. No lifeguard. No deck chair. Nothing. And his cuts ached.

But the *place* that made the vacation a vacation remained the same. After all, the shade was cool, the sand was soft, and the sound of the breakers could have been a soothing accompaniment to the scene. That is, if it were not overlaid with Flint's gasps and wheezes of pain as Kaskil tended to his wounds. Jack felt his reverie broken and turned to see Flint lying facedown in the sand with Kaskil crouched over his back, squeezing out a lime onto their comrade's angry red welts. He could practically hear the wounds sizzling. Flint's fists were balled and his face was red.

"*Fuck you, Kaskil*," he managed, his muscles taut and quivering.

Jack walked over to them. "Kaskil," he began, smiling apprehensively. "What are you doing to him?"

Kaskil looked up at him. Another lime was wedged between his teeth; he spat it out. "Lime juice. It's a natural disinfectant. Haven't I taught you anything?"

"Guess not."

He nodded to Jack's wounds. "You want one?"

Jack looked at Flint and grimaced. "I think I'll stick with saltwater."

"Suit yourself." He paused and flicked his eyes to the side. "Keep watchin' the beach, will ya?"

Jack saluted him. "Sir, yes sir."

The minutes ticked by slowly. The waves rumbled. The palm fronds swayed. Jack looked up and down the beach and into the soft blue haze of noon, but saw not a soul. Flint cursed as Kaskil poured his canteen out onto his patient's back. Keeping his eyes on the beach, Jack finally asked, "You gonna' tell us what Leto told you, Flint?"

Flint pounded his fist against the sand as Kaskil bound his wounds with the moistened remnants of his old shirt. "Augh — *fuck!*" he hissed. "Yeah, yeah . . . in a minute . . ."

"That hurt?"

Flint clenched a handful of sand and watched it drain through his fingertips. "I have learned the true meaning of pain, Jack."

Once Kaskil was finished, Flint rose gingerly to his feet. He glared at his doctor. "I think I'd rather get infected than have you operate on me again."

Kaskil rolled his eyes. "You're welcome."

Flint ignored him and looked at Jack. "All right," he began, wiping the sweat from his brow. "I'd take it with a grain of salt, but here's what he said..."

Flint told them all he had heard from their former commander. He spoke in a voice heavy with doubt and dripping with amusement, as if he were repeating a silly tale intended for children. He seemed to take none of it seriously. When he was finished, he let out a dry chuckle and shook his head. "But it's nonsense."

"What a nutjob," Kaskil scoffed. "Off his rocker 'til the end."

Jack furrowed his brow. Things were coming together in his mind, like the last pieces of a puzzle that had once been indistinguishable yet now looked so obvious in their placement. His story should have surprised him, but somehow left him more satisfied than shocked. It was an answer to his questions. A confirmation. What had transpired between Leto and Jack's would-be killers outside the Fort now made perfect sense. So did Tom's seeming forgetfulness. It disturbed him, but it made sense all the same. "So . . . the Outsiders . . . they're body-snatchers?" he said, matter-of-factly. He searched for a better word. "Shapeshifters?"

Kaskil laughed at him. "Oh, you really believe that? After all Leto's done? You're gonna' take what he said as the truth?"

"Come on, Jack," Flint chided him, raising an eyebrow. "Don't fall for that shit. He just lost his mind."

Jack frowned. "Listen, guys; after all we've seen, does that really seem too far-fetched? Really?" He looked at Kaskil. "I mean, just last night you were attacked–"

"Yeah, yeah, the radiation did funny things to animals. I've seen plenty of two-headed turtles, believe me. That thing was probably just a mutant."

Flint chimed in with: "Lemme' remind you, Jack, that right after Leto told me all that, he started whipping me with the metal end of a belt and ranting about how he wanted to *absorb me* . . . so, like I said, grain of salt."

Jack crossed his arms. "Don't you two remember the girl in the tree? The fact that the outsiders *coincidentally* started vanishing *right* when the Captain and Leto started acting funny, and that Silas denied any of them were gone? Weren't you two a little . . . I don't know, put off?"

Kaskil shrugged. "I was put off, yeah, but that was it. I'm not saying I trust them. Hell, especially not after they tried to ice you. But they're not magic. That's impossible."

"What about Silas's wound, huh?"

Kaskil chewed his lip. "Maybe there was more than one of him. I don't know."

Jack scoffed. "Seriously?"

"Listen, the world's a fucked-up place, and we've all seen how fucked-up it can be, but what you're saying is nuts. A body double's the *only* explanation."

"Oh yeah? Explain the fact that they didn't eat or drink a single thing the entire time they were with us. Tell me that's not unnatural."

"It was. But, then again, that cat that jumped me was pretty unnatural. I'm telling you, it's just the radiation. It messed with their– their D.M.A., or whatever it's called."

"Maybe they're mutants, too," Flint offered. "Maybe they . . . I dunno', need less food and water to keep going. It makes sense."

"Yeah, mutants."

"Exactly!" Jack urged them. "They're mutants . . . and– and, they can assume the form of another being. They started 'vanishing' because that's exactly what they were doing. Like the Wildcat in the tree. Like The Captain. Like Leto. They need to take on new consciousnesses to keep alive!"

"I don't know, Jack," replied Flint, smirking. "Like Kaskil said, I've seen a lot of crazy shit in my time, but that's ridiculous."

Jack smiled. "So all those mutants from the radiation *aren't?*"

"They are," Kaskil told him. "But that makes sense. And shapeshifters don't. Shapeshifting isn't possible. *Period*. It's something in children's books. The fact we're even discussing this is just plain stupid."

Jack grabbed handfuls of his hair. "Kaskil! Didn't you see how Leto caught on fire like that? Come on! That doesn't just happen!"

"Maybe it does."

"Are you guys really this thick?" Jack cried, and spread his arms. "All I'm saying is that it's not that hard even for *me* to believe, after what I've seen. And of all people, you two should have been the first ones to 'fall for' what Leto told Flint."

Flint narrowed his eyes. "You're saying we're stupid?"

Jack shook his head. "Paranoid. Reasonably. Now, *I* feel like the paranoid one."

"Well, you are."

"Well, I should be."

Kaskil shook his head. "I just can't believe it all. It's silly. Ridiculous."

"After what we've seen? After what you've said? God, all the evidence is laid out right in front of us. Can't you see it?"

"I'll believe you and Leto," Flint promised Jack, smiling, "when I see one of 'em transform."

He and Kaskil laughed, and Jack clenched his jaw. "So, what do we do?" he said sullenly. "Huh?"

"Stay put," Kaskil told him, "until Flint heals up enough. Then, we go in, and we torch 'em."

"The Outsiders?"

"Yeah." He narrowed his eyes. "Every man, woman, and child."

Jack nodded, concealing his slight perturbation at Kaskil's words. "Yeah. Shapeshifters or not, they're a danger to our folks." He put his hands on his hips. "But that's a sloppy plan. And what'll the others think? Where's our evidence?"

Kaskil was in the middle of another sentence when, over his shoulder, Jack spotted movement. Not a hundred paces from where they stood, the fronds of the ground palms atop the bank were rustling. And not from the wind.

"Down!" he hissed, throwing himself into the sand behind a piece of driftwood. "Someone's coming!"

Kaskil hit the deck, and Flint did, too, only much slower, and with his teeth gritted. They kept their bodies pressed flat to the ground, only the tops of their heads showing above the log. Jack drew his knife and gripped it tightly. He could hear the other two breathing.

After some apparent struggle, a man popped free from the undergrowth and slid down the bank. He blinked in the sudden onrush of daylight. He carried a rusty machete, and was dressed in an old, tattered set of military fatigues. His face was unshaven; his hair wild.

"A bandit," Kaskil muttered excitedly. He twisted his head to Flint and drew his blade. "Stay back. I can take him."

"No!" Jack whispered. "Wait!"

"Wait for what?"

Jack bit his lip. "He might leave."

"So? He's fair game." He moved to rise, but Jack stopped him.

"Cool your bloodlust." He looked Kaskil dead in the eye. "He's a man, too."

Kaskil glared at him. "I'll whack whoever the hell I want, Jack."

Then, a rustling from above. One of the palm trees that arced out over the beach started to sway and bow as if some invisible hand was throttling it. The Bandit looked up, disquieted. There was something concealed amidst the fronds. They trembled. One fell. Suddenly, they parted. In a blur of motion, a figure in white dropped from them and landed squarely atop the bandit, forcing a shocked cry from his throat. Both crumpled to the sand. Jack and his comrades looked on, bewildered, as a fair-haired girl in a tattered white blouse straddled the bandit and pinned him to the ground. Her face was twisted in a predatory mask of fury.

"It's the girl!" Kaskil gasped. Jack said nothing and watched, fascinated.

Before the Bandit could even fight back, she sunk her teeth into the soft flesh of his throat, sending viscous jets of red arcing through the air. She snarled and licked her lips. The Bandit struggled only for a moment, twitched, and went limp, giving in to his grisly fate.

"*Holy shit*," Flint breathed.

But the girl wasn't finished. She got off the bandit's chest and crouched behind his head, which lay at an unsettling angle in the sand. For a moment she simply gazed down longingly at her kill. Satisfied. She bowed her head to his scalp. Then, as Jack watched through horrified eyes, her teeth began to *grow*. They stretched. They sharpened. The process took only a matter of seconds, and in no time the space between her gaping jaws was crowded with long, hideous, daggerlike fangs that protruded from her gums at nightmarishly abstract angles. Jack blinked in disbelief. But the horrible teeth were still there. She could hardly close her mouth. Jack felt his breath catch in his throat and he pressed himself flatter to the sand. Kaskil and Flint were wordless.

The girl's bloodshot eyes roamed back and forth over the beach for a moment as if she could sense she was being watched. Jack's lungs sealed themselves. Then, satisfied that she was alone, the girl brought the points of her hedgehog of teeth to the man's skull, and sunk them in. His cranium split like a cantaloupe, sprinkling tiny rubies onto her mane of golden hair. She snarled and bit again. More of his skull gave away. Then she dug in her fingers, ripping away flesh and bone as easily as clay until his still-throbbing brain pulsed in her hands. Long strands of drool quivered from between her rubbery lips. Her tongue, long and forked, snaked out and caressed the brain. Jack felt his stomach twist and lurch.

She began to eat.

It was not a lengthy process. Her teeth seemed almost to have a mind of their own. They twisted and oscillated within her swollen gums as her jaws gnashed the brain into an indistinguishable pink pulp. She devoured it as eagerly as a starving tramp devours a loaf of bread, drool and blood soaking through her fingertips. Jack vomited quietly through his own fingers. Some of it oozed from his nose, making his hurl again. Kaskil elbowed him. He gurgled with disgust.

Then, as she finished the brain, her teeth shrunk back to their former size, and she licked her hands and lips. She stood. Her front was stained with a grisly tie-dye of red and pink. With her hands outstretched from her sides, almost Christ-like, she tilted her head back and lifted her eyes to the sun. She looked straight at it.

That was when her flesh began to shift.

It started as a mere prickling beneath her skin, as if a thousand tiny flies were trapped just beneath the surface and were fighting to break free. She seemed to be in pain. Tendons stood out on her neck and a moan emerged from between her bared teeth.

Then it happened. He skin cracked. Twisted. Slid. Ravines of crimson muscle gaped everywhere where her flesh was showing. There was no blood. She screamed and screamed in an agony so profound that it sent a chill slithering down Jack's spine. Made him almost pity her. She fell to her knees in the sand. Her arms and legs jerked and convulsed, and her head snapped back and forth. Her bones were dancing, writhing within her. Her skin seethed and bubbled and squirmed and curdled like boiled milk. Still she shrieked. Her hair fell away into the sand, and new, black locks punched free from atop her head. She convulsed once more, twice, gave a final, strangled cry, then fell silent and still, facedown in the sand.

They watched in fragile silence.

Her head snapped up. Jack's heart skipped a beat. She was no longer *she*.

The bandit rose slowly to his feet. Gnashed his teeth. Flexed his neck side to side. Flexed his arms and legs and twisted his abdomen and ran his fingers over his own naked skin, basking in the raw, electric sensation of inhabiting that reborn flesh. That resurrected form. He grinned a broad grin and looked to the sun. His eyes did not blink. He gave a sudden laugh like a breaking glass, turned, and loped away into the forest.

And he was gone.

Chapter Twenty-One

Jack, Kaskil, and Flint stared on into the distance for what felt like an eternity. The breeze murmured its dissent. The waves, ever whispering in the distance, seemed somehow apathetic to it all; rubbernecking bystanders who came, ogled, and moved on. Jack's eyes were glued to the spot where the once-girl-now-bandit had vanished. He wiped his mouth. He felt shell-shocked. Dizzy. His guts twisted with the cold aftershocks of what he had seen.

"Jesus," Jack uttered breathlessly.

A beat passed. Then, slowly, Kaskil got to his feet. Jack looked up at him. He met Jack's eyes. It was not the piercing gaze Jack was used to. Kaskil's face, typically so animated, now looked hollow. Limp. He ran a hand down his face, letting his fingers pull at any loose skin they could find. He shook his head.

"No," he said simply, voice barely audible. "Fuck this."

Jack stared into the bushes for a moment longer, then stood. He said nothing.

Flint, wincing, got up and looked at him. His features were poised in stark bewilderment. But unlike Kaskil, he looked more impressed than anything, as if he'd just witnessed a volcano erupt from an unsafe distance. He gave a short little grunt of a laugh and put his hands on his hips. "Did . . ." he began. "Did we just see . . . ?"

"Yeah," said Jack. "Yeah, we did."

Kaskil kept shaking his head. "No, no, no."

"Guess it'd be redundant to say you told us so," Flint snickered humorlessly to Jack, and his face seemed to relax. He stroked his stubble. "Then again, I did hear it straight from the horse's mouth. Jesus Christ. Shit."

Jack only nodded; kicked some sand. He couldn't unsee it. He couldn't unthink it.

Deep breath.

Kaskil puffed out his cheeks and blew a sharp breath. He ran the fingers of one hand through his hair, while the other white-knuckled his knife. Both hands were quivering.

"Something eatin' you, Kaskil?" Flint asked him.

Kaskil turned and looked at him. He looked like he'd been slapped in the face. "Yeah, Flint. There is." He gesticulated violently, unable to find the words. "What the *fuck* was that?"

"Exactly what you think," Jack told him, running his tongue over his teeth. "Exactly what I told you."

"Fuck you, Jack." He turned away. "No. This– this is bullshit. I can't. No. No, no, no . . ."

"Scared?" Flint laughed.

"Yeah, I fucking am!" He whipped around and looked hard at them, blue eyes sizzling. "And I'll tell you what–" He held up his finger. "–we're getting off this fucking island right fucking now. Yeah. I'm not hangin' around here one goddamn second longer with that– that fucking skinwalker on the loose."

"What, you wanna' leave?" Flint scoffed. "Just like that?"

"I do. Yeah."

Flint arched an eyebrow. "You know we've been sleeping right next to them for days, right? The Outsiders?"

"All the more reason to get the *hell* out of here!"

Jack felt like he could vomit again–

(her skin was moving)

–but said, quaveringly: "I thought you weren't afraid of anything, Kaskil."

Kaskil's jaw muscles twitched. "Listen, you two. I've seen a lot of crazy shit in my time. I've *done* a lot of crazy shit. Hell, bring me the greatest warrior on earth, and I'll fight 'im. But that?" He shook his head rapidly. "What we just saw . . . that was *ungodly*."

Flint shrugged. "Storming the beach at Santa Monica was a hell of a lot scarier."

"You tellin' me you aren't shitting yourself right now? Really? Did you have your eyes closed when she– when she *changed?*"

"I don't think so."

"And you're just *cool* with that?"

"No," Jack admitted, meeting his eyes. He felt shaky. "I'm pretty fuckin' scared, Kaskil. I've never seen anything so– so *disgusting* in my life. But–"

"*But* what, Jack?"

Jack hesitated for a moment. "But what about the villagers? Our people?"

"What about them?" Kaskil spat.

"We can't just leave them to– to . . ." He searched for the right word. "Be . . . *taken*. We can't abandon them." His eyes rested on a seashell, and he shrugged. "It's not right."

"Listen to Jack," Flint said, crossing his arms. "We're Guardsmen. We're supposed to protect them no matter what. It's our duty to keep them safe."

Kaskil's face was slowly turning red. "Are you out of your mind? No! No . . . I– I am not messing with that *dark magic* bullshit!"

"But they're defenseless," Jack argued. His conscience weighed too heavily to carry, even though he knew full well he was probably a lot more scared than Kaskil was. The thought of them being attacked made him sick. "Think of the kids. We can't just–"

"I saw the devil today. I saw him."

Flint palmed his face. "Jesus, Kaskil. Grow a backbone."

"Why should I put myself within a ten-mile radius of that fucking monstrosity? Huh?"

Jack set his jaw. "Because it's the right goddamn thing to do."

"*–you cowardly, unempathetic bastard,*" Flint muttered, shaking his head.

Kaskil ignored him. "Look, Jack. How long've you been with us? A month? Who are the villagers to you? I'll bet you don't know most of whom you call 'your' people. They're not your friends. Your family." He narrowed his eyes. "Why are they so important to you, Jack?"

Flint sighed loudly. "Stop beating around the bush, Kaskil. You're just scared. Strap a set on and shut up, will ya?"

But Kaskil words, though callous, rang surprisingly true somewhere deep inside Jack. he was wordless for a moment, then said, simply: "They aren't, really." His eyes drifted to the sand. "You're right. They're not my friends. My family."

"Then *why* won't you listen to your instincts?"

Jack blinked and looked at him. "Because I swore to protect them. And because they're relying on me to do that." He quirked his mouth to the side in thought. "It doesn't *matter* whether they're close to me, Kaskil. They're just *people. Good* people. And they don't deserve to die, or– or worse. They just don't." He paused. "And . . . well, I'd give my life to protect them."

"But *why?* Why *you?*"

"Because–" But his voice broke, and he froze mid-sentence. Looked at the ground. Something was gnawing at his insides. Something with icicles for teeth.

Suddenly, the presence of a pair of dog tags under his shirt became obvious.

He had thought the memories would only return at night. Had willed it. Only in nightmares would he have been forced to relive them. That was how it had been. But then, standing before Kaskil and Flint, they all came flooding back. It felt like there was a cinder block wedged into his ribcage. He felt his lip quiver but managed to bite back the tears.

Kaskil scoffed in irritation and turned away towards the water.

Jack struggled for a moment before finding his voice. "I never, uh–" He cleared his throat. "Well, I never told you guys why I joined the Guardsmen."

Kaskil rolled his eyes. "Jesus, Jack, this better not take all day. That *thing's* still out there, and–"

"Shut up, coward," Flint snapped at him.

Jack let his eyes wander across the sand for a moment before hauling them back up to his comrades. "Uh–" He cleared his throat. "Guess I never spoke about how I got here. Or, uh, about these." He pulled the dog tags out of his shirt. "Not mine."

Flint raised his eyebrows. "I thought you didn't have any secrets."

Jack smiled a little. "Well, I mean . . . I do. I guess." He looked down at the dog tags. "I had a brother." The word *had* was like an arrow to the guts. "His name was Eli. He served in the war." Jack chewed on his words for a moment. "He was the bravest man I ever knew. And, well . . ." He drew a shaky breath and began. "We were on a ship. A small ship. It was called the Albatross. Onboard were us, the Captain, and a few others; all refugees. We were on our way to Hawaii, 'cuz Hawaii didn't get bombed. But then . . . then there was the storm." He looked at the ground for a moment. "I don't remember much, but what I do remember is . . ." He bit down hard to keep his tears from flowing. "Sorry."

Flint smiled. "It's okay. You don't have to–"

"I do." He cleared his throat. "Eventually, well, the ship broke its back, and we were all in the water. It was pitch dark. Freezing cold. I climbed on top of the pilothouse, but only a second later it went under, and the roof drifted off. It barely held my weight." He swallowed. "Then I heard Eli. I remember turning my head and seeing him in that awful yellow glow of the mastlight, struggling there, only a few feet away. He couldn't swim. He called out to me. I reached out. But the raft tipped. Then I knew . . ." He swallowed. ". . . I knew if I tried to reach him, I'd fall off the raft and drown. I can't swim. And he kept getting carried further and further away. Pretty soon it was too late." He bit his lip. "Then, the last light went out. It went dark. And he was gone."

Jack bowed his head. The tears, thankfully, did not come, but his heart was a pincushion for nails. His chest physically ached. For a moment he just stared at the ground, but when he looked up at Kaskil, the blue-eyed man met his gaze.

"That's why, Kaskil," Jack said. "That's why I joined the guardsmen."

Kaskil said nothing.

"'Cuz I knew it was my fault he drowned. I could have reached him. Let him have the raft. But I didn't. I was selfish. And because of that . . ." Jack blew out a breath. "Now he's dead, and I have to live with that for the rest of my life."

Still, Kaskil was silent.

"I can't let it happen again, Kaskil. I can't let these people die. They're counting on me. They're counting on *us*. I *have* to protect them." Then, with his eyes drilling into Kaskil's, he solemnly added, "If we don't do something — if *you* don't do something — they'll end up just like my brother."

A long, clockless moment passed. Then Kaskil spat a single word: "Fine." He shifted his jaw back and forth before adding, "Fuck, I'll do it. I'll fight for them."

"Say it," Flint ordered. "Say I was right."

"Shut up, Flint."

"*Say it.*"

Kaskil ground his teeth together. "I'm not a coward. I don't gotta' tell you nothin'."

"But you won't run?" Jack asked him.

"No."

The corner of Jack's mouth rose a centimeter. He felt acres less afraid. "I knew you were better than that."

Kaskil kicked the sand. "Cut it out, okay?"

Flint clapped him patronizingly on the back. "There's that backbone."

"Don't touch me."

Then Flint looked at Jack and put a hand on his shoulder. "I'm sorry," was all he said, and Jack dipped his head in thanks.

A period of silence followed. It was long, but strangely unawkward. All three seemed content to listen to the murmur of the sea and the chatter of the songbirds. Despite his pain, Jack felt as if a great weight had been lifted from his chest.

Kaskil spoke at length.

"So, what's the plan?" he asked. "What'll we do? How will we save them?"

There was a quiet beat.

"We can't possibly take the Outsiders on alone, even with all the torches we could hope to carry. They'd overpower us." He crossed his arms. "We need something better."

Jack sniffed and blinked, a sudden thought occurring to him. He almost didn't speak it. He knew what they would say. But once he thought the thought, it seemed that it was the only thought he could think. "I've got something. A plan. It might not work, but . . ."

"Hey, it's *something*. Let's hear it."

Jack smirked, then looked side to side. "Not yet. Let's wait until night falls. The woods have ears."

Chapter Twenty-Two

It was evening, and the sky was gray, dim, and dull. Clouds obscured the field of blue that had graced their sights only a few hours before. It was as if the Outsider's transformation had disturbed not only them, but had provoked disapproval from the heavens as well. The air felt still and hot. The breeze of the morning was gone. To the untrained observer, it would shape up to be a calm night. Jack, though, knew better. A storm was coming. He could feel it. Not just in the evening's stuffy warmth, but in the sort of constrained, galvanic quality that hung all in the air around him, and that he sucked in with every breath.

Jack had put off telling Flint and Kaskil about his plan for as long as possible. He knew they wouldn't like it. They'd hate it, in fact. They'd fight back. But, as Jack knew after deliberating on his decision for hours and hours in an attempt to find a better plan, it was their only option.

Even though Flint's wounds were nowhere near healed, he had made clear his design to take part in rescuing the surviving villagers. As night fell, he was again groaning in the sand as Kaskil cleaned his bandages and started a fire, over which they turned seagull carcasses on sharpened sticks. The sight of the meager breasts made Jack's mouth water. He hadn't eaten in a day and his stomach was rife with hunger pangs.

As for their strange firestarter, it had come from a plastic crate which was zip-tied shut, keeping it unexposed to the elements of the Pacific which carried it, by chance, to them. Inside was a stack of flat, square cardboard sleeves. Jack recognized them as records. On the front of each was printed a black-and-white image of four men, their faces half-cast in shadow, and above them, a row of blocky letters cried out at them in colorful proclamation. Jack hadn't read in years, and it took him a moment to understand what they meant.

"*Meet the Beatles*," Kaskil read aloud, lifting out one of the record sleeves and tossing the disc aside into the sand. It was worthless and useless in such a time. "I wonder if they were any good."

Jack knelt in the sand beside him, feeling a little twinge of desire in his chest. He missed listening to records. He missed Rock n' Roll. "Guess we'll never know."

"I guess not."

"They look like a bunch of faggots to me," Flint grumbled.

"Well, jeez," Kaskil replied and tossed the sleeve into the fire.

There was a long pause. "You gonna' tell us about your plan, Jack?" Kaskil asked him, his voice laced with impatience. "Night's a-wastin'."

"Alright," Jack replied warily. "It's . . . well, it's a bit crazy."

Kaskil grinned broadly, his pointed teeth gleaming. "I think I can handle crazy."

"You won't like it."

"Maybe I won't. Maybe I will. Only one way to find out."

Jack swallowed and nodded, dreading what he was about to tell them. But he had to do it. And he did.

When he was finished, he glanced back and forth between Kaskil and Flint, frantically searching their faces for approval. There wasn't much to be found. Kaskil looked pale with fury, his brow drawn; Flint stared at him quietly and intensely.

"You're joking," Kaskil uttered. "That's suicidal. That's . . . no. I won't. I can't."

Flint looked up at Jack. "Jack, to hand over everything we've fought for is . . . well, it's unthinkable."

Jack's mouth felt dry. "I know. But I've thought about it. A lot. It's our only option."

"Our only option?" Kaskil sneered. "Really? The most *insane* option is our only option?"

"Why don't you come up with a better plan?"

"Any plan is better than that! Dying isn't what bothers me — to ally with those monsters, I . . ."

"I know they're evil," Jack admitted.

"They fucking are."

"And I know the land is ours."

"Ding-ding-ding. Right again." He pinched the bridge of his nose. "Three years we've lived here, Jack. Three years. It took a year alone just to build that damn Fort. To throw it all away, to have all that blood, sweat, and tears go to waste — it's hard. Too hard."

"Kaskil's right, for once," Flint offered with a sigh. "This plan of yours means sacrificing more than our lives, which I think you know is exactly what would happen. It means putting the axe to everything we've done to make a life for ourselves on this island. Putting the axe to our morals. To the dignity of our fallen comrades." He sighed again, then went quiet.

Jack looked at the sand, then back up at Kaskil and Flint. "I hate it, too. What we have to do. Really. I know the price."

Kaskil's piercing stare met his own, deep and blue and harsh. He looked disgusted. "I've lost friends to them, Jack. Close friends. I've seen . . ." His voice trailed off, and he looked back at the fire. "And the Island . . . it's our home. It has been for so long. To do this would be harder for me than it would be for you."

Flint nodded solemnly. "I'll give my life for my people in a heartbeat," he affirmed. "But like this . . . well, I'm worried we'll end up wasting our lives before we can make any difference."

"We won't be wasting our lives if we try."

"But there's no way this will work."

Jack stood and clenched his jaw. "Listen, I'm tired of arguing. Do you two want to save our people or not?"

"We do, but–"

"If you've got a better plan, I'd like to hear it now."

"Well . . ." Kaskil began. "The other guardsmen. What about them?"

"We can't count on them. The Outsiders would have taken them over the villagers, considering they're the ones who can fight." He paused. "Got anything else?"

Kaskil and Flint were silent.

Jack turned his knife over and over in his hands, watching the flames dance across its polished surface. "I'm sorry, guys. I know this won't be easy after everything you've been through. But you know we can't take them on alone."

Kaskil prodded the coals.

"You know it's our on–"

"Yeah, Jack!" Kaskil snapped. "I know. I heard it the first time."

"Will you come with me?"

"You're gonna' go alone?"

"If I have to."

"You can't."

"Try and stop me."

Kaskil chewed his lip. "We'll die, won't we?"

Jack nodded solemnly, staring into the fire. "I think so. But I'd rather die than be responsible for another wasted life." He looked up at Kaskil. "Will you die for them?"

"Like I said, it's not really the dying that bothers me."

"I know. All the same, will you follow me?"

Kaskil stared at him for a moment, and Flint did the same. Jack could feel their gazes drilling into him. Then Flint stood and walked up to him. He put a hand on Jack's shoulder. "I'll do it," he said, the corner of his mouth lifting ever so slightly. "It's my duty. It's crazy, but it's my duty."

Kaskil laughed suddenly and Jack and Flint looked down at him. He was chuckling and grinning more of disbelief than of mirth, his teeth flashing in the firelight. His stormy blue eyes met Jack's. "Oh, what the hell. What's wrong with me?" He rose to his feet. "Count me in."

Jack smiled, relief draining the breath from his lungs. "Thanks, you two," he told them. "For trusting me. Really."

"Of course," Kaskil replied, clapping him on the shoulder. "You're a good man. You're a brave man. Shit, you've saved my life twice now. Your plan might be stupid, it might go against everything I've done and fought for on this island, but I'll follow you to the grave if it means protecting our people. I promise."

"So do I," Flint told Jack. "I'll stand by you."

Jack grinned, feeling light and tall. "What are we waiting for, then?"

Just then, as Jack looked back to the fire, he caught a flash of movement to his left. It was just beyond the reach of the flames' flickering glow. A writhing of many parts not unlike the skin of the fair haired girl as she had transformed. Jack's gaze flicked to the squirming thing, and he felt his stomach turn a bit as he recognized it.

Thereopoda Cunifera.

"A centipede," he said aloud, scooting subconsciously towards the fire. Not a pace from where he sat, that tiger-striped insect was legging its intricate way across the sand towards them, its long antennae twitching like lovecraftian whiskers.

Kaskil sat up a bit. "Larry," he said, with a faint smile. "I wonder how he found us."

Flint jumped backwards at the sight of the creature. "Keep that fucking thing away from me."

"He won't hurt you."

"You don't know that."

Jack turned to Kaskil, brow furrowed. "Wait, how do you know it's the same one? The same one from the Fort?"

Kaskil rose, walked around the fire, and scooped up the centipede. It ambled along down his forearm, pincers flexing absently. Kaskil scrutinized it for a moment before saying, "Yep. It is."

"But how do you know?" Jack repeated.

"He's missing one of his back legs. Besides, his stripes are a little different. They're broader than usual."

"Gosh, I thought *I* was the entomologist."

Kaskil set Larry down in the sand. "It's weird that he's here. I thought they had smaller territories."

Jack stared at the bug, stroking his stubbled chin. "Yeah, so did I."

It was then that a strange, disturbing thought came to him. He stood and looked at Kaskil, then back at the centipede. "Do you think . . . ?"

Kaskil cocked his head, then widened his eyes. "Oh."

Jack ran his tongue over his teeth. "How long do you think it's been . . . listening?"

"Long enough."

Jack turned to Flint. In a tense, measured tone, he said: "Flint. Toss me one of those records."

With a grunt of pain, Flint did so, and Jack caught it. He frisbeed the disc off into the distance, then pushed the edges of the sleeve together so that it resembled a gaping cardboard mouth. "Kaskil," he whispered. "Catch it again."

Kaskil nodded gravely and crept after the centipede, which was making its quiet way towards the trees. It seemed to notice him and picked up the pace, its legs a maddening blur, its body twisting like a snake, but Kaskil pounced and pinched its abdomen between his fingers. It curled its body in an attempt to bite Kaskil, but could not. Kaskil scurried back to Jack and dropped the insect into the waiting cavern of the record sleeve. Jack pinched it shut. His skin crawled as he sensed it wriggling about inside the sleeve, but that feeling was coupled with one of relief.

"Sneaky little bastard," Kaskil chuckled. "I thought I smelled a rat." Flint rose laboriously to his feet and approached them. "We should burn it. Now."

"No," said Jack quickly as another thought crossed his mind, this one taking the unsettling edge off of the last. "We can use this to our advantage with the Bandits. Trust me." He looked between the eyes of his companions. "Remember when Leto burned? Didn't you see how his body . . . changed?"

Kaskil shook his head, but Flint gave a single nod. "Maybe," he said. "If it improves our odds, I'd take the bug."

Jack looked down at the record sleeve. "And if . . . *Larry* . . . tries to change before that, he gets the torch." The insect's squirming died down a bit, and Jack smirked in satisfaction, knowing he'd get the torch one way or another. He folded the top of the sleeve over and shoved it down his shirt.

"Speaking of fire," Kaskil said to Flint, "you've got the lighter?"

Flint nodded and pulled the glistening little gadget from his pocket. "Roger."

"Try not to lose it — I've had that thing for years. Besides, it might come in handy later."

"We should eat," Jack said, cutting in. "The sun's about to go down."

The other two concurred silently, and they ate. The meat was sour and far overcooked, but to Jack nothing had ever tasted better, and he demolished his seagull.

When they were finished, final preparations were made for their respective parts of the plan. Flint took his trusty wristblade, the lighter, and a machete. Jack and Kaskil kept their own weapons concealed under clothing, and, of course, brought the record sleeve with their evidence sealed within. They extinguished the fire and made ready to split up.

"Ready?" asked Jack.

Flint nodded once. Kaskil looked to him, back to Jack, and the corners of his mouth lifted in the razor-sharp grin Jack had been expecting. "Let's do this."

"Remember the rendezvous point," Jack told Flint, putting a hand on his shoulder. "Plug any bandit who's not with us. Plug any Outsider, period."

Flint dipped his chin. "Good luck, you two."

"Same to you."

Kaskil saluted him. "Godspeed, my friend."

Flint gave them a final once-over and marched stiffly off into the forest to the North. Jack and Kaskil watched him go, turned, and headed off towards the East. Above them pealed the first drumbeats of a thunderstorm.

Chapter Twenty-Three

Jack and Kaskil trudged through the jungle with their hands held over their heads. Each carried a knife tucked hilt-first into the waistbands of their trousers, but, as Jack had made clear, it was imperative that they not use them. They were to come in peace, as brothers of the apocalypse.

The sky boiled as they headed east, blocking out the moon and stars, rendering the jungle black as pitch. Jack felt strangely unafraid. The bandits were ruthless, savage; this he knew, but he also knew that they were human. They bled and hurt the same as he did. Maybe, just maybe, he and Kaskil would be spared. Maybe, just maybe, the bandits would show some honor. There was at least a slim chance. And if they were to die, then so be it. He doubted he would survive the night no matter what happened. There was not much to be afraid of at that point; he had committed to that course of action and was determined to follow it until the end. Death was inevitable. It would come for him sooner or later, he reasoned, a looming shadow like the clouds above. One day or night, it would envelop him in the inky folds of its cloak. Jack was sure that this night would be the night. He felt strangely at peace with it all. To go down doing something noble gave him no qualms. It was an age-old ideal; romanticized; quite literally 'to die for'. To be a hero, even if nobody remembered him; for the latter part didn't really matter. He would die nobly for himself and for those he fought to protect. That was all.

Furthermore, after what he had seen at the beach, bandits were no longer the reason he feared the jungle. Larry continued to writhe within his cardboard prison.

"We come in peace," called Jack at intervals into the undergrowth. No longer did he feel his breath hitch when he raised his voice outside the walls of the Fort. For once, he actually wanted — needed — the bandits to hear him. "We wish to speak with your Rafe. We are unarmed."

Kaskil grumbled uneasily to himself as they walked. Jack looked over his shoulder and saw that he had drawn his knife. "Kaskil," Jack said sternly. "Put it away."

"Thanks, mom, but I know them better than you."

"And I know that the only way we're going to save our people is if we look unassuming. You want to save them, don't you?"

Kaskil said nothing.

"So, put it away."

Reluctantly, Kaskil did as he was told. "If one of 'em makes a move," he grumbled, "I'll turn 'im inside out."

"I'm sure you will."

Just then, Jack felt the top of his boot catch on something. It felt like a root. He tripped, caught himself awkwardly, then looked down. It was not a root. It was a cable. In an instant, a checkerboard of rope sprung up from the greenery at their feet. They barely had time to cry out before the net closed upon them like a giant baseball mitt, and within the blink of an eye they were dangling, crushed together sardine-like, the net swinging lazily to and fro above the trail. Kaskil cursed loudly and struggled against the ropes. Jack swallowed his racing heartbeat and drew a shuddering breath, rough rope pressing against his face. Kaskil was like an electrocuted rat beside him.

Stay cool.

"Cut it out, Kaskil," Jack snapped at his struggling companion. "We're not dead yet."

"We *will* be if we don't get the f–"

"I mean it, Kaskil. Don't ruin our chances. Do you want this plan to work or not?"

"Yeah, but I–"

"This is perfect. They'll come running any second– stop cutting the ropes! I can feel you doing it!" He craned his neck to look at Kaskil, his features grim and hard. "Just don't move. I'll do the talking, got it?"

Kaskil spat through the netting. "Fine."

"Well, well, well," came a sudden voice from below, dripping with uncanny amusement, making the two of them jump. "Whadda' we have, here?"

Jack looked down. Two bandits stood beneath them, spears in hand, their faces crowded with hair, their clothing tattered and mud-spattered. They bore grins the color of dirt. One — the speaker — prodded the net with his speartip. He was short and thin; his companion was broad and tall.

"Outsiders," said the latter with a sinister glint in his eyes. The word struck Jack as hysterically ironic; stingingly accurate.

"Trespassing on our hunting grounds," the former tsk-ed. "As if they hadn't taken enough of it already. Scum." He thrust the butt of his spear into Kaskil's leg and drew a furious grunt from between Kaskil's teeth.

"Listen," Jack barked down from above, trying to keep a waver from his voice. "We're not trying to take your game. All we want is to speak to your Chieftain– I mean, your Rafe."

They laughed. "Good one," the former said. "Haven't heard that before."

"We're unarmed," Jack furthered. He felt his stomach twinge a bit at the lie. "Just cut us down and take us to him. We don't want any trouble."

"Oh yeah?" the latter said, crossing his arms. "Why don't we kill you right now, huh?" He prodded the net with his pike. "Stick you right through. Maybe spitroast 'ya. How 'bout that?"

Jack's mind raced for a witty answer. Found one. He swallowed, then said, "I wouldn't try that, if I were you."

"Oh-h-h!" the former crowed. "How courageous!"

"I mean it. We aren't alone."

"What's that supposed to mean?"

"There's others. Oher guardsmen from our tribe. They're everywhere." He pointed to the left and right. "Hiding, in the trees; with bows. Try anything and you're dead."

The bandit chuckled. "Yeah? How do we know you're not lying?"

"There's only one way to find out."

The Bandits exchanged a skeptical glance, then let their eyes wander about the greenery around them. The latter looked back at Jack, his lips thin. "Listen, Outsider. We'll cut you down and take you to our Chieftain if you can give us a good reason why you want to talk to 'im."

"It's a bargain," Jack explained. "A deal."

"Like . . . ?"

Jack told him their course of action. The Former's eyebrows went up, and both Bandits looked at one another again, then shared a handful of whispered words.

"That's a big favor to ask," said the latter. "A very big favor."

"Don't you want that land back?" Jack pressed, his heart racing again.

Please please please please please

The former exhaled. "Yeah. We fuckin' do." He paused. "But you gotta' call off your men, first. Then you come down."

Jack lifted his gaze to the trees and addressed his imaginary warriors. "Stand down," he commanded, and gave a quick signal with his fist that was entirely improvised. Kaskil gave a dry snicker.

The Bandits looked at each other a final time, then back to Jack. "All right," said the former simply, and slashed the net open. Jack and Kaskil fell to the ground like rocks. A dull burst of pain radiated from Jack's rear, and he cursed through his teeth. The Bandits aimed their spears at Jack and Kaskil; ushered them to their feet, giving each an experimental prod. Hands went up over heads. Jack could hear Kaskil suck his teeth in poorly-masked rage as the spearpoint poked the small of his back. Jack prayed to whatever god was watching him that they wouldn't be searched for weapons. Thankfully, they were not, and with the bandit's spears hurrying them along, they were marched to their enemy's stronghold.

Chapter Twenty-Three

They walked for what seemed like hours. Sweat trickled down the back of Jack's neck, and though mosquitos attacked him with vigor he didn't dare swat at them. He'd held his hands over his head for so long that the muscles in his shoulders were beginning to quake. Just as it seemed their captors were playing some sort of trick on them, a jagged window of sky appeared up ahead, and the sound of crashing waves reached their ears. The trail emerged quite suddenly onto a precipice — the East Cliffs, as Jack recalled. Before the trail turned and followed the treacherous border between land and sea, Jack snuck a look over the edge. It was an incredible drop. Far below, waves the size of houses threw themselves passionately against the island's rocky flank, scattering themselves into twisted fingers of white froth each time only the process again and again. The wind was picking up, driving them on at their eternal masochism. A speartip probed Jack's side and he stumbled along.

The cliffs curved outwards up ahead towards the ocean, and from his vantage point Jack could see a stark yellow glow emanating from midway up their rugged haunch. He figured it must be their destination. *What a place,* he thought. It all seemed very fitting.

They teetered on the brink between life and death for perhaps a mile more before the trail angled gently away from the jungle, left its red dirt behind, and struck out along the cliffside. Ahead of them lay a long, unwinding descent towards the Bandits' Stronghold. Jack felt a serpent of fear coiling around his spine as his boots met uneven stone. The became narrow and steep; their party walked with one foot in front of the other, and one hand against the cliff for meager support.

In places the rock was slick from the spray of the relentless sea. Jack slipped once or twice, adrenaline exploding in his veins each time. He wondered, despite himself, if the trail was natural or if it had been hand-carved. Either way, it was as amazing as it was terrifying.

The descent felt like five miles; it took up a quarter of one. Jack was glad when the path broadened into a wide shelf and torch-wielding guards greeted them with cold complexions. The sight of fire was another small comfort.

The ledge grew and grew as they headed towards the yellow glow — now radiating from around a corner — that had been visible from so far away. Jack's gut was twisted by the strong hands of anticipation.

They rounded the bend, and were faced by the Stronghold of the Bandits.

Jack stopped dead in his tracks at the sight of it; nearly smiled in awe before being prodded along by his escort's spearpoint. He had never seen anything like it in his life.

The Stronghold rested within a deep cut in the face of the cliff; a notch nearly a hundred meters deep, by Jack's estimate, and perhaps fifty from the sea to its head. From the floor of the cut to its window to the night sky, more shelves just like the one they had crept along to reach the Stronghold striped the cliff face. Some were narrow; others wide; but the Bandits had taken total advantage of these natural conveniences. All glowed with the lights of a thousand torches, and were bustling with their occupants. Campfire smoke swirled up in great sheets and melded together to form a cloud of hazy blue that hung over the whole settlement. Shelters constructed of wood, animal hides, and various flotsam crowded almost every ledge from the floor of the slot to twenty meters up. A few dwellings simply consisted of an overturned skiff or rowboat. Rickety ladders led from ledge to another like those neolithic settlements Jack had seen long, long ago in school books. And from one wall of the slot to the other, rope bridges of equally unsound appearance were strung. Between Jack and the sky high above him was a spider web of rope and planking that went up, up, and vanished into the darkness and woodsmoke. Bandits of all ages and sexes scurried from one wall to the other along these twisting walkways, their stays secured higher up than the torchlight could betray, and though Jack thought at any moment one may come crashing down and spill its screaming occupants onto the hard stone floor of the slot, nothing of the sort happened. The Bandits seemed confident in the security of their infrastructure, however unorthodox it may be.

As for the Bandits themselves — Jack couldn't help but feel a bit surprised. Though he'd only been on the Island for a month, his view of the bandits as a whole was well-formulated; they were savage and ruthless people whose only purpose seemed to be that of destruction. Hell, he'd been attacked by one himself. But now, looking up at the Bandit's lofty home and its many residents, they felt suddenly, jarringly *human*. For the first time, Jack thought of them not as enemies but simply as people. People with lives and emotions and families. There were not only those hated soldiers dwelling here, but women, children, elders . . . and not all were dirty or barbaric in appearance as he had so long pictured them. But it was the sight of their youngsters that twisted his perception the most. Perhaps, just perhaps, the man he had killed had been a father to one of those kids. Perhaps Jack had created an orphan.

For the first time in a week, he felt the cold, slimy grip of remorse.
It hurt.

But there was little time to dwell on such emotions, for their party was moving on, proceeding across the floor of the slot and towards the real centerpiece of the Bandits' Stronghold. It loomed over them from the headwall of the cut — an airplane. Some sort of jet, Jack guessed, from the sweep of the vine-draped wings and its cylinder engines. The plane was positioned to that those engines faced Jack and his companions. Its wings were crumpled against the walls of the cut, and long scratches were dug into the rock from the its floor to its summit. The tail was buckled upwards against the headwall along with most of the fuselage, and the nose had been removed entirely, along with all of the aircraft forward of the wings. A cross-section of the fuselage revealed a row of seats, and an intricate stack of rocks leading up to them; a sort of half-pyramid of stone steps. In the center of the row, in a leather seat decorated with seashells, animal skins, and skulls — *maybe*, Jack thought, *those of old guardsmen* — the man whom they had come to see presided over his kingdom. The Rafe.

Jack had only heard of this title in passing; only caught it in short, clipped, bitter sentences like droplets of lime juice in a cut. To hear it gave him the chills. The leader of the bandits, Jack thought, must have been the fiercest and most ruthless of men. After all, he was feared by every member of Jack's tribe whether they wanted to admit it or not. The man was almost respected. To see him, to be in his presence, was breathtaking.

The Rafe was a man equally as striking as his title. Like the Captain and Leto, he was black, but the leader of the Bandits' skin was so much darker; so much richer. It made his eyes, a lighter shade of blue than Kaskil's, stand out in a way that made Jack's skin prickle as if grazed by a thousand needles. They were twin stars gleaming from the dark, silky expanse of space that was his flesh. Jack looked quickly away from them. Those eyes reminded him of Caine and Lester.

The Rafe was also a large man. Jack figured he was a few heads taller than even Flint. But unlike Flint, he was far from lean. The Rafe was truly dense; not obese, but sturdy, robust, with arms and legs like tree trunks and a chest like a barrel turned on its side. A dense, jet-black beard crowded the lower half of his face. He wore a great flowing cape fashioned from the gold-and-black skin of a Leopard. Atop his bald, glistening head, a tall headdress rested, patterned intricately by the vibrant colors of bird feathers. His torso was bare, and on it rested an equally ornate necklace of dyed animal fangs. Across his bulging biceps were blue armbands woven with the skulls of small animals. With one of his arms he held a lance, its obsidian tip glinting in the torchlight, feathers hanging from its shaft like a rainbow.

Sharply contrasting this attire was that of his lower half. On his legs and feet, he wore old military trousers and simple combat boots. They were partly decorated, but surprisingly plain. If it were not for these articles, The Rafe would have reminded Jack of one of the Mayan Kings of old.

Heads turned as their party walked towards him. People of all ages and colors and sexes went quiet. The silence spread like the first ripples of a soon-to-loom tsunami. It was a silence that made Jack's stomach squirm and his head hang. Made him want to sink deep into the solid rock beneath his feet. Never in his life had he felt more vulnerable, more exposed; here, deep within the home of his supposedly sworn enemy, who could destroy him at any second, whom he had come to make a deal with. It took everything he had to keep from shaking.

The air was taut as the stays supporting the countless walkways above their heads. Jack swallowed. The tension had to be released.

That was when the jeering began. Hundreds of people were suddenly hollering for his blood. For his head. For his skin. His heart was in the back of his throat. It was both terrifying and humiliating. Jack bowed his head and willed himself to take slow, measured breaths and block out the awful orchestra of hatred. Kaskil's face was read with fury. A few Bandit soldiers ran up to them, weapons drawn, but their escorts blocked the attacks and told them off. The men retreated, furious. Rocks and sticks were thrown. Jack was hit by a few. He tried not to flinch and kept his eyes to the ground.

"Silence!" boomed a voice.

A few of the voices calmed.

"*Silence!*"

The Bandits quieted in an instant. Jack looked up. The Rafe had risen to his feet, his piercing eyes now locked onto Jack and Kaskil.

"Leon, Gunnar," he addressed their escorts. His voice was like thunder. "Why have you brought me these Outsiders? Why have you not slain them?"

Some of the Bandits raised their voices again, but the Rafe raised his fist and they petered off.

The former and the latter stepped forward. "Rafe," said the former, "they wish to speak to you."

The Rafe arched an eyebrow. "Oh?"

"Yes," said the latter. "They came willingly, and are unarmed."

At this, the Rafe cocked his head slightly to the side. "And what is the business of these Outsiders? Why should I not have their skulls?"

The former and the latter stepped back and held their spears against Jack and Kaskil's sides. "May they speak?" said the former.

"Yes," replied the Rafe.

Jack looked at the leader of the Bandits. Those eyes... He opened his mouth, but found that words evaded him. A rill of sweat ran down his back.

"You may speak," the Rafe commanded him, his voice louder this time.

Jack cleared his throat. "Sir, we–"

"Address me as Rafe."

"I'm sorry... Rafe. We have come to make a deal with you."

He grinned dryly. "A deal? You wish to make a deal?" He lifted his head and voice and exclaimed: "The Outsider wishes to make a deal!"

Jeers and laughter erupted, and Jack felt his cheeks go warm and his gaze fall flat on the stony ground. "Yes," he managed. "A deal."

The Rafe raised his fist again, and his people quieted. "And what is this deal, may I ask?"

"We are in danger," Jack told him. "*You* are in danger. Something evil has come to the island." He paused. "I have come to raise an army."

"You hope that my men will fight for you?" he chuckled. "After all you people have done?"

Jack could hear Kaskil open his mouth, then restrain himself. Jack went on. "Do you believe in the supernatural?" he asked the Rafe, looking him dead in the eye. "Do you believe in . . . dark magic?"

The Rafe considered this. "It depends. What exactly are you trying to tell me?"

"Our tribe has been . . ." He searched for the right word. ". . . infested. By creatures. Creatures that can assume the form of any living thing they please."

The bandits within earshot of him snickered incredulously, and the Rafe smirked. "And why should I believe you? Why should I put faith in this silly claim?"

"Because," Jack told him, grim-faced, "I can show you." He reached into his shirt and drew forth the record sleeve. "Bring me a torch."

The Rafe knit his brow, then complied, jerking his chin at one of his personal guards. They descended the stone steps and passed a crackling torch to Jack. The centipede squirmed inside its confines, sensing danger. Jack felt a pang of dread as he held the flame, knowing that if the insect did not transform, he and Kaskil would surely be killed. Perhaps Leto hadn't changed as he burned. Perhaps it was just a trick of the light. Perhaps all they'd see was a sizzling bug.

He swallowed, whispered a silent prayer, and lowered the flame to the record sleeve.

It burst into flames and he dropped it. The centipede darted out from the sleeve, wriggling and twitching and flailing its legs as it burned, and the Rafe leaned forward in his seat, features drawn in curiosity. Jack was frozen, watching.

Suddenly, a ball of flame erupted from where the centipede should have been, and when the firestorm dissipated something that looked both human and disturbingly inhuman lay twisting and screaming on the stones, its body wreathed in fire, its form somehow unclear, somehow chill-inducing despite the heat. Gasps and cries erupted all around him, and the Rafe drew back a bit.

A sheet of bloodred flame shot up into the smoky air before the flames burned out and nothing but a pile of ash remained where the shapeshifter had once writhed in its death throes. A deafening silence hung over the stronghold, interwoven in the swaying catwalks above, swirling amidst the smoke.

"What have I seen?" the Rafe spoke at length, his tone heavy with bewilderment.

Jack found his voice, and replied, "That was one of them. One of the Shapeshifters. Fire kills them." He swallowed. "There are more. Many more."

The Rafe met his eyes. "So you ask for my men to combat these . . . things."

"I do."

"Why," the Rafe spoke, his voice heavy with something that could have been wonder, could have been fear, "should I give them to you? Why should I let them die for a people who have taken so much of our land and game? Why?"

"Because," Jack explained, "if they will die, they will die not only for us, but for you, and for your tribe. These creatures are a danger to us all — not just to us. They are a danger to every man and beast on this island."

"Our stronghold is impenetrable."

"No, it isn't. They can take the form of any living thing they want. One of your guards, for instance; or even an insect like the one I set on fire. They *will* bring ruin to your people."

The Rafe stroked his chin. "An army . . . of how many?"

"One-hundred," Kaskil spoke up. "No. One-hundred and twenty-five. That should do it."

The Rafe puffed out a heavy breath. "Quite the number."

"Yes. It is. But if they've started to multiply, then their numbers could be much more than just twenty. There could be sixty. Eighty. Who knows."

"If we ever want to bring them down," Jack added, "we'll need to outnumber them. They're fast. They're tough. And they can transform in a matter of seconds."

The Rafe nodded slowly in contemplation. "You said, Outsiders, that you had come to make a deal. If we fulfill our end of the bargain, what do we get in return?"

"Your land," Jack told him. "You get it back. All of it."

A murmur rose amongst those within earshot. The Rafe smirked, his curiosity piqued. "Oh?" he chuckled. "You two are certainly full of surprises tonight."

"We aren't lying," Kaskil interjected. Jack could tell those were difficult words for him to speak. "The Island's all yours."

"And what will *you* do?"

"Simple," said Jack. "We'll leave."

More excited mutterings.

"No more fighting. No more bloodshed. We'll be gone in a day."

The Rafe eyed them with suspicion. "This is big talk," he said. "Big promises."

"We'll keep them."

"But *will* you? How do I know you will keep this promise? Tell me, Outsiders, what authority do you have to make this deal at all?" He scoffed. "How can I be sure you aren't planning to lure my men out into the forest to be ambushed? Does your Chieftain even know you were sent?"

Jack's stomach sank. He ran his tongue along the backs of his teeth, mind racing. This was somehow unexpected. "Our chieftain is dead."

The Rafe barked a quick, harsh laugh. "Dead? Then who has sent you? Who is your leader?"

"I am," Jack blurted, looking the leader of the Bandits dead in his icy blue eyes. He could feel Kaskil side-eyeing him. "I am the new Chieftain of my people."

The Rafe smiled and narrowed his eyes as murmuring erupted once again. The guards nearest to them snickered in disbelief. "You?"

"Yes."

"You're so . . . young."

Jack said nothing, only looked at him, unblinking.

The Rafe went on. "How can you prove this?"

"I can't." He paused, then said, "But I *did* prove one thing. I proved to you that we're all in danger; great danger; every one of us. And I proved that I was willing to reconcile this . . . this awful, *pointless* conflict between our people that's wasted so many lives." He gestured around the cavern. "That's left so many children fatherless." He crossed his arms. "If you have any honor, that should be all the proof you need."

The Rafe scoffed bitterly. "Don't talk to me about honor."

"That's all I have to tell you."

There was a long pause. The Rafe whispered something to one of his aides, and they engaged in a hushed, terse conversation. Jack shifted anxiously back and forth from heel to heel, perspiration moist on the pads of his fingers. This was it.

"I will need some time," the Rafe spoke at last, "to make my decision."

"There's no time!" Kaskil nearly shouted. "They're gathering their forces tonight. They plan to take your fortress. We can stop them before they even begin to advance."

Jack smiled in his mind. A lie. Yet, again, another unprovable lie. He wondered if their plan may succeed after all.

The Rafe raised his eyebrows. "You wish to destroy them tonight?"

Jack nodded. "Yes."

"And if I send my men to fight for you, then will you give us back the land that rightfully belongs to us?"

"If we don't," Jack promised, "see to it each and every one of us is killed. We're men of our word."

The Rafe went silent for a moment. He stroked his beard; exhaled. Looked to his aides. They said nothing, seeming to shrug with their eyes. The leader of the Bandits rose to his feet, spear in hand, and addressed the inhabitants of the stronghold.

"My people," he began in a voice that had no need for a microphone. Every soul in the place went dead quiet. "These men, these Outsiders, have shown us evil tonight. They have shown us the unnatural. They have shown us something that, so they say, will bring an end to us all if we do not stop it. They ask for our manpower. For our soldiers. They ask us to help them fight against this evil." he paused, allowing the denizens of the slot to murmur amongst each other in a great symphony of hushed tone not unlike that of the crashing surf outside. "But they have also come to make a bargain. If we choose to fight for them, and for us all, they will grant us something we have desired for so long: our land." The murmurs grew louder. "They will give us back the hunting grounds that were once rightfully ours, that they brought so much suffering upon us to take. They will give us back our birthright. And they will leave. In peace, they will leave.

"They will give us this if we comply with their one demand: that our soldiers fight with them to bring an end to this black magic, black magic that threatens to destroy us all. So I ask you, my people, what you make of this — do we want peace? DO WE FIGHT?!"

The cheers were deafening. A clamor unlike anything jack had heard erupted from all three walls of the Stronghold. Jack went weak-kneed, relieved beyond belief, and Kaskil clapped him on the back. A smile spread across his face and his held himself with his hands on his knees. They'd done it. It had worked. The Bandits would fight. The villagers he had sworn to protect could be saved yet.

"My people have spoken," the Rafe said to Jack, grinning. Then, the leader of the Bandits turned to his soldiers and addressed them. "Men! Arm yourselves with torches and muster in ranks! Prepare to move out!"

"Here we go," said Kaskil to Jack, grinning.
Jack nodded. "Here we go."

Chapter Twenty-Four

A clap of thunder sounded. Lightning spilled across the leaden sky, lighting up the forest floor in a flash of blue. A wildcat screeched like a woman. *Ominous*, Flint thought to himself, and smiled.

He moved quickly towards his destination. This westward trail had been largely surrendered to nature, but nature would not surrender to him. Fingers and tongues of green reached out to stop him, to tangle him, entrap him, but he tore through the frail impediments with ease, taking long, sweeping strides through the foliage. He whisked his machete to and fro, slicing at stems and leaves and vines.

It felt good to be alone. Both Jack's pitiful optimism and Kaskil's petulance had started to wear on him, though the latter much more than the former. They would die, all of them, and he did not care. He owed it to the people he had sworn to protect. Besides, he knew deep down that he had lived long enough. Seen enough. The concept of death did not really faze him as much as it once did.

His wounds stung, too, and as he often found, it was better to be alone with his pain.

Eventually the great bulk of the Fort soon loomed above him, at first a vague shadow against the murky sky, then silhouetted starkly by a flash of lightning. Sentries paced along the catwalk, pikes in hand. Flint ducked low into the foliage. He crept along, colors dancing on his retinas from from the flash, machete gripped in a palm oddly devoid of sweat. The undergrowth gave way and he darted across the short clearing to the stockade. Pressed himself against the logs. He considered the North Gate, but decided on the South, instead, as it was closer. With his back pressed to the stockade, he shuffled silently towards his point of entry.

He reached the final corner and peered around it. Two guards watched over the gate. Flint recognized them as old friends — John and Axel — *but*, he realized with a small pang of bitterness, *is it really them?*

Flint approached the gate in as nonchalant of a manner as he could; raised a hand in greeting. "Evening, boys," he said in a low voice. The two guards crossed their spears to block his path. He stopped. This was alarming — they should have recognized his voice. He put a fist to his chest and said, "It's just me. Flint."

One of the guards — John — retracted his spear. "Oh," he said, tone vaguely hesitant. "Sorry, brother, I didn't recognize you."

Flint ambled slowly up to them. He fingered the lighter in his pocket, then stopped. No — that would cause too much of a stir. Anyhow, he had to be sure, so he looked to one, then the other, and asked, "Tell me, you two. What was the name of the ship we came here on?"

The guards exchanged a wary glance. "That's an odd question, Flint," said John.

"Yeah," Axel concurred. "Why do you ask?"

Flint shrugged. "No reason. I'm just curious if you remember."

Again, the sentries looked at one another.

"Well," John began. "It was a long time ago . . . things like that just don't stick around in my head."

"I've got nothin'," Axel told Flint, shaking his head.

Flint furrowed his brow. "All right, then. Was it a big ship, a small ship . . . ?" He smiled. "Surely, you two aren't thick enough to have forgotten that."

"Uh," began John. "It wasn't *too* big, but I might not be rememberin' right."

Axel stroked his stubble. "Yeah, pretty small. A fishin' boat, right?"

Flint smiled humorlessly and passed his gaze over the eyes of the sentries. They had come to the island on old troop transport — the Luzon. It was nearly the size of the Titanic. He swallowed.

"Really, boys?" he asked again.

The first gave a small shrug, looking confused. "It was a long time ago."

Flint clenched his jaw and nodded. This would be hard. They looked so much like their former selves; spitting images; hell, even their voices were so accurate it was hard to tell that they were just excellent impressions. But these creatures were what had killed them, killed men he had considered closer than brothers. His pity drained at this thought.

It had to be done.

In a single lighting-fast motion, he swung his machete through the throats of both, spattering deep-red blood across the weathered planks of the gate and silencing their vocal chords. Then he punched his wrist blade into their guts while they were stunned. They crumpled against one another, croaking and sputtering, eyes rolling back. Flint clipped his machete into his belt and retracted his wrist blade, then grabbed each of the sentries by their collars and dragged them away into the undergrowth, one by each of his powerful arms. Flint left their twitching, gasping bodies in a heap and covered them with foliage. He hoped that fire wasn't the only thing that killed these creatures.

With the dirty work out of the way, Flint slunk back to the gate, wiped the blood off it with his sleeve, and slipped inside.

What he saw inside alarmed him.

It was empty. Well, nearly empty. He saw more and more sentries and villagers he recognized as he glanced around the interior of the fortress. But their population had been halved — maybe more. And worse, the number of Outsiders seemed to have doubled. As he squinted through the darkness, he saw both children and adults that he did not recognize, and many more of them, too. Before this had perplexed him, but it all made sense now.

They had multiplied.

It was doubtless, too, that no guardsmen remained. Of course the Outsiders would have targeted the villagers' defense force, as, after all, it was their leaders who were first to go. Flint felt anger spike in his nerves as he pictured the fate of his old comrades. But, he reminded himself was here to get the villagers first, and the guardsmen — or whatever remained of them — second. Those without the skills to defend themselves were the first priority.

Flint took a deep breath and walked silently to the clustered hammocks of the nearest family, making sure to keep within the shadows and out of sight from the sentries above. There was a father, mother, and their three children — the Brewers. They had come to the Island with Flint aboard the Luzon. He knew that the children, especially, would recall that great ship. He knelt beside the father's hammock and tapped him on the shoulder.

The man stirred and opened his eyes. He gave a small start, but Flint pressed a finger to his own lips in warning. "Bandits are coming," he whispered. "They'll attack soon. I'm here to take you and your family to safety."

The man sat up, alarm in his eyes. "I can fight," he professed.

"No," Flint said firmly. "Leave it to us. But first I've gotta' ask you something." He leaned in close to the father's ear. "What was the name of the ship we came here on?"

"The Luzon," he replied, a bit perplexed. "Why?"

"It doesn't matter. Wait for a moment."

Flint repeated this process with his wife and each of the three children, making sure that none heard the answers of the others before they were asked. All passed the test. Flint told them to gather their belongings, arms, and a canteen of water, then quietly shepherded the group out through the gates and down the beach.

Once they were sufficiently far enough from the Fort, Flint directed them to a palm-draped hollow at the edge of the sand and told them to stay put.

"If I don't return when morning comes," he said, "and if Kaskil or Jack don't, either, then we're dead." He put his hand on the father's shoulder. "Take care of them."

The man nodded solemnly.

Flint left them and returned to the Fort.

He repeated the process a second time, and a third, each time going unnoticed, and each time seeing to that each family member passed his test. He took each of the families to the same place, so that they would have the advantage of safety in numbers if attacked.

Each time he entered the Fort and saw the Outsiders sprawled in their enclosure, he felt his blood boil, and wondered if he could take them alone. Surely, he could not. And it would bring ruin to their scheme. He recalled his task, and returned to it.

There were not many remaining families. Perhaps only a handful. He approached the fourth — the Changs — and crouched alongside the mother. She did not panic when he told her of their situation, and passed his test. So did the father. Feeling relieved, he woke their single child, a girl of fourteen, and whispered his question into her ear.

She paused for a moment. "I– I don't remember," she stuttered, looking at the ground. Flint's stomach sank. "It was a big ship, I don't remember its name. Why?"

"It doesn't matter," Flint assured her. What she had followed her initial statement somewhat quelled his doubts. After instructing them to bring water and their weapons, he led the Changs quietly towards the gate. They slipped through and started down the beach. Once they had covered a distance that was safe by Flint's estimate, he faced the girl.

"Give me your arm," he commanded softly.

She looked at her parents, who said and did nothing, then back to Flint.

"Trust me."

Tentatively, she extended one pale, unmarked forearm. He drew the lighter and flicked it open. The flame was shockingly bright in the darkness. She flinched away, but Flint grabbed her arm.

"This might hurt a bit," he told her, then looked to her parents, "but it's important. I can't explain right now. I've just got to do it." He looked at the girl in her big, scared eyes. "Be brave."

She looked at him for a beat, then nodded. He brought the lighter down to her arm, hovering it over the skin. His hand was quivering. He drew a breath and steeled himself.

With a flick of his wrist, he brushed the flame against her skin.

The girl winced, but that was all. That was all. Flint exhaled and stowed the lighter, feeling a wave of cool relief wash over him.

Thank God.

"Who goes there?"

Flint spun and faced a shadowy figure drawing close across the sand. Tom. The once-guardsman halted before them and pressed the tip of his spear to Flint's chest.

"What's the meaning of this?" he demanded, his eyes flicking over the Chang family's worried faces. "Did you take them here?"

Without hesitation, Flint looked Tom dead in the eye and said, "They're sick, Tom. Indigestion. I'm here to escort them to the latrines."

Tom flared his nostrils and lowered the spear. His gaze was steely. "Why isn't this gate guarded?"

"I don't know," Flint snapped. "I wasn't put on guard duty."

"What exactly *was* your detail today, Flint? No — I think a better question is where the *hell* you, Kaskil, and Jack have been for the entire day." He narrowed his eyes. "Where were you three?"

Flint turned briefly to the Changs, and said quietly: "Head East, follow the tracks, find the others."

The mother and father nodded, and they left.

"I asked you a question, Flint," Tom barked.

Flint stepped up to him. They were nearly the same height, but while Flint's massive bulk could put most men cowering in his shadow, Tom was unflinching. Flint smirked.

"Here's my answer, Tom."

Flint jabbed his wrist blade up into Tom's throat, choking his cry, and with his other hand flicked the lighter open and pressed into the wound.

There was a flash not unlike that of an atom bomb as Tom erupted. To Flint's night-adjusted eyes, the inferno was brighter than anything he'd ever seen. It was like staring into the sun. He shielded his gaze with one arm and backed away, as Tom's writhing body folded into the sand and fizzled out like a ruby-red firework. Then he turned and took off running for the Fort while Tom's glowing ashes settled into the sand.

Chapter Twenty-Five

Men trailed behind Jack and Kaskil like a long line of ants as they traversed the cliff and marched into the jungle. The Rafe plodded along ahead of them, his torch like a flickering lantern in the darkness. Jack couldn't help but glance over his shoulder every twenty paces or so, for he had no reason to trust these former enemies, and doubted that the Rafe would do much to stop them if they made a move against Jack and Kaskil. Jack couldn't keep the image of a spearpoint pressed to his back out of his mind. He could almost feel the bite of the obsidian tip. Kaskil seemed just as on-edge.

Both of them knew, deep down, that the only way for their mutual distrust to dissipate was by being attacked by the Outsiders. It was grim truth, but a truth all the same. Jack wondered if they would be fighting their old friends. Wondered if Flint had taken all of the villagers to safety. Though he knew it would have been his worst fear just a few days prior, Jack hoped and prayed that the Outsiders had taken the remainder of the guardsmen. He hoped to God that they would not be set upon by their former comrades. He prayed he would not have to kill one of the men who had served alongside him in defending their people.

Either way, they faced nothing but danger from there on out. If they were not killed first by the Bandits, then the Outsiders would surely rip them to shreds, consume their identities, and inhabit their forms. Jack's guts felt heavy. Pangs of fear like blows of a fist traveled through his abdomen every few breaths. His quivering palm was slick at the hilt of his torch, which crackled and spat and cast an eerie yellow light on the looming greenery all around them. He carried his knife, too, though he knew its effect would pale in comparison to the fire.

But it's not my *knife.*

He smiled a bit at the irony of it all. Here he was, going into battle alongside his former enemies, one of whom he'd slain, the weapon of which he now carried. It was darkly comical.

Though it didn't help much, he tried to tell himself to be brave. He knew Eli would have. Of course he would have. Jack shook his head slightly as he felt the light metallic clink of the dog tags around his neck. No; he would never have the courage his brother had. But he didn't have to. He knew he could fight the Outsiders, he'd fought them before and won. And this time, too, he was equipped with the one thing that brought them sure destruction. Why should he be afraid?

But he was. He *was* afraid. It was an emotion that simply couldn't be pushed down. All he could do was let it run through him, let it torture him, let it try to tear him apart, and know that it couldn't kill him. It was just a feeling.

He accepted it, swallowed, and kept marching on into the night.

There came a sudden rustling from up ahead, past the Rafe's hulking silhouette and the sickly glow of his torchlight. A shadow flitted from the bushes. A man. Jack's breath caught in his throat. The Rafe held up his fist and prodded his torch forwards in order to illuminate the interloper as murmurs arose in the line of Bandits behind them. The figure stood motionless in the middle of the trail for a second longer, then darted away. It was as if they were never there.

The column moved on, slower now, ears cocked and eyes scanning the foliage for signs of the enemy. Jack's heart thrummed in his chest. Though some part of him hated to admit it, his fear was slowly being replaced by a sort of grim excitement; an anticipation.

"They know we're coming," Kaskil whispered to Jack, his gaze cold. "They'll be ready."

Jack nodded. "Good," was all he said.

He, too, was ready.

It wasn't long before they reached the last straightaway in the trail that led to the Fort. Torches flickered in the distance. Jack drew a quivering breath and steeled himself. If he would die, he would die, and he would die for good. He was in the hands of fate now.

As their small army drew closer and closer, the black bulk of the stockade and the catwalk's silhouette came into focus, lit yellow from behind by torches inside the Fort. A lone figure stood atop the wall. He was unarmed and alone, standing with his legs slightly apart, his arms dangling at his sides from broad shoulders, and his head held high. The cutout was unmistakable.

Silas.

The trail widened as they got closer. Jack and Kaskil strode up alongside the Rafe and their army followed suit in jagged lines of three. Looking back, a python of fire snaked back into the forest from whence they had come. They came to a halt twenty paces from North gate and Silas's silhouette. The gate was open. Inside, the Fort looked completely empty, yet lit bright as day. Fresh tracks were torn into the mud under the gateway. Jack knew this could mean only one thing: troops had been awoken, mustered, and deployed. He readied himself for the inevitable.

"My friends," Silas greeted them with a sweeping wave of his arm. "Welcome."

"We don't want your hospitality," Jack called up to him, brow heavy, voice strangely unfaltering. "And you won't be getting ours for a second longer, Silas."

Silas chuckled. "How impassioned. I do hope you and your friends haven't come to start any trouble."

"You'd be disappointed."

As if on cue, an arrow was loosed from a Bandit's bow and it found its mark in Silas's shoulder. He barely flinched, ripped it out, and tossed it aside. A murmur of disbelief arose amongst the bandits. Jack glared on.

"What a shame," Silas lamented, tsk-ing. "Such violence. Such a craving for blood. For death." He sighed. "I despise violence, Jack, I really do. After all, I'm sure you know that I lead a people who are above all other things *peaceful*."

"'Peaceful' my ass," Kaskil laughed humorlessly. "I've seen what you and your kind do. It's barbaric. It's unnatural. Tonight, it's all over."

"Oh, it's only just beginning."

"We'll destroy you," Jack told him. "We'll burn you all."

Silas's smile faded. "Why, Jack? Why must you and your comrades resist the inevitable? Resist His will?" He reached out his hands. "Why won't you join us? We don't have to fight. We will forgive all the wrong you have done against us." He smiled almost warmly. "Become one with us."

"Never," Jack spat. "You're insane if you think we would."

"But you could be great!"

"I don't want to be great," said Jack. "I just . . . I just want to be *human*."

"I can show you what I mean," Silas promised, his tone suddenly heavy and stiff. "I can show you the true form of greatness."

Jack's lips went thin. "You're outnumbered, Silas. Give it up."

Silas ignored him. Silently, methodically, he began to strip off his clothes. He stood naked atop the catwalk and grinned down at them. "Prepare yourselves," he announced. "Prepare to see our true plan for humankind."

As Jack watched in quiet horror, Silas began to transform.

His teeth elongated. His skull elongated. His fingers elongated. Claws shot from their tips; curving scimitars of keratin. His skin peeled away like wallpaper and blood-red flesh and muscle gleamed in the firelight. A second pair of arms burst from his sides in a spray of blood and stretched outwards from between his shattered ribs, growing long and spindly. So did his other limbs. Their joints snapped and crackled as they shifted sickeningly out of place until his arms and legs finally bent in two places like those of a spider. His spine twisted and cracked and shot upwards a foot. He screamed and screamed all through it, but his shrieks rang less of agony and more of revelment. He *enjoyed* it. The Bandits moaned in terror.

Then it was finished. His crimson lips peeled back in a revolting grin, baring his twin rows of dagger-like teeth. "Now, do you see?" he growled in a voice unnervingly similar to that of Silas's. "This is our true form. Behold it." He spread his twin pairs of lanky arms — if they could be called arms. "Don't you crave to inhabit this flesh? To inhabit the flesh of others? To inhabit any form you please."

"All I crave is to watch you burn," said Jack.

"Why must we play this game?" Silas snarled. "Must all this blood really be shed tonight? You can become part of something greater. Part of mankind's future."

Kaskil's lip curled. "I'd rather die than be part of your future."

"Very well." Silas bowed his glistening head as if in thought. His long claws twitched at his sides. "You leave me with no other option."

Jack's heart skipped a beat. He gripped his torch and his knife.

Silas threw back his head, strings of saliva quivering between his fangs, and screamed a single command.

"*ATTACK!*"

Chapter Twenty-Six

All around them, the jungle exploded with motion as Silas's soldiers burst from the foliage and surged into the line of bandits from either flank like twin tidal waves. The corridor of greenery leading to the Fort became an alleyway of chaos. Cries and roars and screams filled the air. Everywhere, bodies and weapons clashed together and crumpled to the muddy ground. Jack could see nothing but a sea of movement all around him. The smell of burning flesh became almost instantaneously overpowering as the Bandits set fire to their enemies and some were immolated themselves.

An Outsider tackled Jack and slammed him to the ground. The Outsider had taken its final form. Its eyes bulged lidless and slit-pupiled from their sockets. Its bare muscles twitched horribly with each movement. A bolt of panic shot through Jack as he realized he'd dropped his torch. The creature snarled and moved for the kill. Its fangs nearly closed around Jack's throat before his groping hand closed around the torch's hilt and he plunged it into the creature's side. He scrambled away backwards as it went up in flame and lay writhing on the ground. A fist closed around his forearm and dragged him to his feet — Kaskil.

"Jack, look!" Kaskil screamed over the din. He pointed frantically to the top of the gate where Silas had been standing moments before. "He's gone!"

Jack looked just in time to see him drop to the ground inside the Fort and lope away towards the South Gate. "That coward!" Jack snarled.

Leaving the din of the battle behind, they tore through the gate and across the barren interior of the Fortress, their torches still clutched tightly and trailing rivers of sparks through the cool night air. The South Gate was still swinging as they slammed through it — and into Flint. Jack toppled him to the ground. Recognizing instantly the identity of his comrade, he rolled off and swept up his torch before it could be put out in the sand.

"The guardsmen," Flint breathed, struggling to his feet with Jack's help. "They've all been taken. All of them."

"It doesn't matter," Jack snapped, grabbing his hand and pulling him along. His entire body itched to run. To chase. "Silas's getting away!"

"Come on!" Kaskil shouted, but they had already taken off running and he sprinted after them. The ferns still swayed where Silas had vanished. They crashed into the jungle, torches blazing, the flames casting eerie orange halos, greenery disintegrating at their legs and waists. They came upon a trail almost immediately, and Jack's light revealed a set of strange, clawed footprints etched into the mud. The prints led off down the path. Wasting no time, Jack and the others followed.

Jack had never run so fast in his life. His killer instinct was bubbling up through his bloodstream, somehow hotter and more furious than it had been when he had battled Caine and Lester. It swirled together with adrenaline until the two were like a riptide of fury surging through his bloodstream. His lungs and legs screamed, but he felt no pain. Or, rather, he ignored it. Either way there was only one thought occupying his brain, and it was Silas — Silas wreathed in flame as he burned, shrieking as his wretched life was seared from the thing he called a body. The Outsiders had taken too many innocent lives, too many of his comrades. Now, their leader would pay. Kaskil and Flint pounded along the trail behind him. No doubt the same thoughts occupied their minds. They were on the hunt. Like the primitive men of antiquity, their instincts had kicked in to the fullest, and the iron surety that their quarry drew nearer and nearer with every step was embedded in the minds of each like the obsidian head of a spear.

The prints did not deviate from the path, leading west; ever west. Were they being led somewhere? A trap, perhaps? These thoughts crossed Jack's mind, but only for a split second. He did not care. Did not think. He wanted only to kill.

He ran.

The jungle began to thin and the ground steepened beneath their feet. Still, the prints stayed true to the beaten mud of the trail. Jack's breathing rushed out heavy and wet. Saliva was plastered in long strings across his cheeks. His heart leapt as he caught a glimpse of movement amidst the scrub ahead. Silas couldn't get away — Jack picked up his pace, hands and feet scrabbling until he summited the plateau.

The sound of breakers was suddenly crystalline. He stopped, panting, his eyes scanning the plateau. Not twenty paces from where he stood was a sheer drop-off to the raging sea far below. Thunder rumbled and a flash of lightning illuminated the scene. The plateau was strewn with boulders; some knee-height, some taller than Jack. He, Kaskil, and Flint formed a circle with their backs to the center and held their torches out into the darkness. Except Jack's torch was the only one with any flame left to speak of. Below, the sea hissed ghoulish incantations.

Crash.

A peal of thunder, and lightning split the sky. A shadowed figure stepped out from behind one of the monoliths. His face was lit up for the blink of an eye, but not long enough. Jack squinted into the darkness. The figure did not move.

"It's over, Silas," said Jack, his tone firm yet sizzling with an electric hate. He started towards the figure who stood like a toy soldier at the edge of the cliff. This was it. Torch held aloft, he quickened his pace. The figure remained motionless. Jack could hear Kaskil and Flint closing in behind him. Their torches had burned out, but their spirits had not. Jack went for the kill.

"Jack, no!"

Jack froze. It was not Kaskil, nor Flint, nor even Silas who had spoken those words. That voice . . . it sent a chill slithering down Jack's spine. He hadn't heard it in what felt like eternities.

"Jack, kill him!" Kaskil urged. But Jack could barely hear him.

Crash. Lightning struck again. The figure was bathed in pale blue light, but this time his face was burned into Jack's retinas even when darkness closed in again like the Red Sea behind Moses. It was unmistakable.

"Eli?" he uttered.

Eli stepped forwards. "Jack," he breathed. "I can't believe it's you."

Jack would have rushed forward, would have embraced him, but something held him back. Was it him? He gulped. "Eli, I . . ."

"You survived." He sounded as shocked as he sounded relieved.

"I . . ." The words escaped Jack, but he managed to catch a few before they slipped away. "I thought you were dead."

Eli smiled. "Here I am."

Jack's breathing became shaky. It was Eli. It was Eli *in the flesh.*

"It's not him, Jack!" Kaskil screamed, his words falling on deaf ears. "It's not him!"

Tears came to Jack's eyes. His lips quivered. "Eli, I'm sorry."

Eli's smile faded.

"I'm so sorry."

"Jack, Burn him!" Flint shouted. He lunged for Jack's torch, but Jack thrust it at him and he backed away, hands held out. "Are you crazy?!"

Jack swung it at Kaskil, too, who drew back with fear in his eyes. He screamed something at Jack. He screamed many things. His voice was hoarse. Jack did not hear. He only turned and stared into the hardened gaze of his brother. Those eyes — if they were an illusion, a front, then Jack's brother may have always been an Outsider.

Eli was silent a moment longer, then said, "Do you know what you did to me, Jack?"

Jack could not speak. An icy fist gripped his guts.

"You left me to die, Jack," said Eli quietly.

Jack's mouth fell ajar. "I– I–"

"You're sorry. I know." Eli looked down. "I'm your brother, Jack."

"I know, I–"

Eli's lip curled. "How could you?"

"I–"

"You betrayed me."

Jack fought back his tears, teeth gritted. His fingers quivered at the hilt of the torch. Flint and Kaskil were screaming, screaming, their voices panicked. "Eli..." he managed.

Eli's eyes darkened. "*You betrayed me*, Jack." He lifted his chin. Lightning flashed, casting his stony features in shadow. His eyes wandered into the distance, then closed. "I don't know why I ever called you my friend." Then opened his eyes. Stared straight at Jack, and said, " I don't know why I ever called you my brother."

Something snapped deep inside of Jack. It was flint on steel; a fire re-igniting.

He'd never say that. Never.

"No," Jack said, looking Eli dead in the eye. "You never did call me your brother." The tears seemed to retreat from his eyes, and he stepped forward. "Because *you're* not my brother."

The imitation's jaws gaped and his eyes went wide. "Jack, sto–"

But Jack's torch plunged into his chest before he could ever finish the sentence. A wail tore from his throat as the flames consumed him and he staggered backwards. Flames burst through his eye sockets, from this throat, from his flesh.

The imitation shrieked. It stretched out its arms, almost Christ-like. For a moment it seemed to hang, suspended in mid-air over the precipice, cloaked in flame. Jack watched through a steely gaze. He felt the heat tightening his skin.

Thunder crashed, lightning spilled across the scene like mercury, and the thing that had tried so hard to be Eli, had tried in vain, fell.

And it was gone.

Chapter Twenty-Seven

The walk back to the Fort, or what was left of it, felt short. None of them spoke. Jack knew he should have expected celebration on the tails of their victory; cheering and back-slapping, but there were none, and he expected none. It was grim. Not anticlimactic, but grim. All were satisfied. There was no call for joviality.

Their task was complete.

They emerged into the clearing where the Fort had once been just as day was breaking. Only a few timbers still stood, blackened and charred like jagged headstones. The bandits drifted, ghostlike, through the ruins. They gathered their dead and heaped them into a small mountain of flesh. Smoke curled up in cold tendrils into the dim blue of dawn. Jack heard Kaskil utter a small groan at the sight of their former home. The three stood there in silence for what seemed an eternity before the Rafe approached them. He was bleeding from a gash in his shoulder.

"You ran," he said. He looked no less betrayed than the Eli-thing had. "You are cowards."

"No," Jack told him, thrusting forth the burned remnants of his torch and tossing it on the ground. "We killed their leader. It's done."

The Rafe looked at him for a moment, flared his nostrils, then looked down. "We, too, found victory. But at a price." He turned and gazed regretfully at the corpses of his soldiers. "Twenty. That was the price." He shook his head. "*Twenty.*"

"They didn't spend their lives in vain," Jack told him, placing a hand on the Rafe's unwounded shoulder. "They did a noble thing."

The Rafe looked at him and sighed. "Yes. But it is hard."

"Nothing is easy."

The Rafe looked at him a second longer. "And you? Will you hold up your end of the bargain? Now that my people have suffered and bled, you could commit no greater sin than–"

"Yes," Kaskil snapped. "We will leave."

"Then we will help you prepare for your journey."

Jack dipped his head. "Many thanks, Rafe."

The Rafe dipped his head in return, scanned their faces once more, and walked away.

Jack and Kaskil helped to glean the battleground. It was a solemn task. Once the bodies were gathered in a funeral pyre, they were set alight. They burned much slower than the Outsiders had. Jack had difficulty letting go of that realization. These were men — human men. Jack and Kaskil bowed their heads and stood as the bodies crumbled to ash.

Flint retrieved the villagers. They were shaken by the sounds that had rung out through the night, especially the children, but none were harmed. There were twenty of them. One for every fallen bandit. The sight of the bandits frightened them at first, but they were soon told the truth of what had happened the night before and their sentiments shifted like the tides.

The Outsider's boat was stocked with provisions. Its kegs of water were refilled, and salted meat was loaded into the tiny hold. Then, the hands of the villagers, bandits, and the three remaining guardsmen guided the little craft down a set of plank slipways and into the shallows.

While some of the villagers searched the remnants of the Fort for their belongings, Jack, Kaskil, and Flint sat in the sand and watched the sun rise over the ocean.

At length, Kaskil spoke up.

"Where will we go?" he said, and looked at Jack.

Jack shook his head slowly. "I don't know." He looked at Kaskil. "Where the wind takes us, I suppose."

Silence returned. Kaskil skipped a seashell out across the lapping waves and watched it sink.

Jack felt a sudden stirring deep in his chest. There was something he had to do before he ever stepped foot from the island, something he should have done a long time prior. It was like a magnet pulling at his heart. He rose to his feet in the sand. "There is one thing I know, though," he said, never more sure of anything in his life.

Yes. It has to be done.

His comrades looked up at him, unspeaking, puzzled. Jack met their gazes and was equally silent. He only smiled.

He undid the clasp on Eli's dog tags and held them up before his eyes, studying the tiny letters impressed into their metallic surface. He held them briefly to his chest. Closed his eyes. Whispered something he'd never remember.

Then, he cast the dog tags into the sea. They vanished beneath the surface in the blink of an eye. For a moment he watched the ripples spread, then sat down between his friends.

They watched the sun rise and said nothing more.

About the Author

J.R. Goodrich is a man with a passion for two things: writing, and the great outdoors. When not busily tapping away on his keyboard, he can be found skiing and hiking in the wilds of his home state, Alaska. He takes inspiration from the striking balance of beauty and danger which can be found while exploring that great landscape. He lives in Homer with an overfed Corgi named Sitka. *The Jungle Never Sleeps* is his first novel.

Milton Keynes UK
Ingram Content Group UK Ltd.
UKHW020757231024
450026UK00001B/82